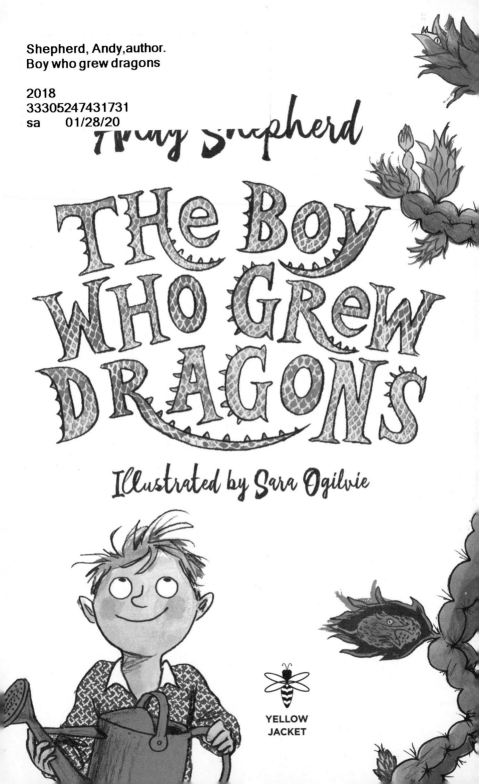

Andy Shepherd

THE BOY WHO GREW DRAGONS

Illustrated by Sara Ogilvie

YELLOW JACKET

YELLOW JACKET

251 Park Avenue South, New York, NY 10010
Text copyright © 2018 by Andy Shepherd
Illustrations copyright © 2018 by Sara Ogilvie
All rights reserved, including the right of
reproduction in whole or in part in any form.
Yellow Jacket and associated colophon are
trademarks of Little Bee Books.
Originally published in Great Britain in 2018 by
Piccadilly Press, an imprint of Bonnier Zaffre Ltd.
Manufactured in the United States of America LAK 0120
First U.S. Edition

10 9 8 7 6 5 4 3 2 1

Library of Congress Cataloging-in-Publication
Data is available upon request.
ISBN 978-1-4998-1011-0
yellowjacketreads.com

For more information about special discounts on bulk purchases,
please contact Little Bee Books at sales@littlebeebooks.com.

For Ian, Ben, and Jonas,
for always believing in dragons—and in me

When people ask me what we grow in Grandad's garden, I think they expect the answer to be cucumbers, tomatoes, or green beans. I don't think they expect the answer to be dragons. But there it is. We grow dragons. And I can tell you this—they're a lot more trouble than cucumbers.

Things cucumbers do *not* do:
Poop in your dad's oatmeal.

Singe your eyebrows.

Make a really cozy nest by shredding
all your mom's alphabetically
ordered recipes.

Leave your underwear (the
embarrassing ones covered in
backhoes) hanging from the TV antenna.

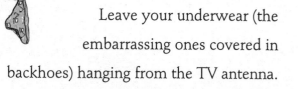

Chase your cat.

Drop cabbages on your cat.

2

Try to ride your cat like a rodeo bull.

Wake you up at 4 a.m. every morning by digging razor-sharp claws into your forehead.

Set fire to your toothbrush WHILE IT'S STILL IN YOUR MOUTH.

Of course, they also don't have scales that ripple and shimmer like sunlight on the sea. Or have glittering eyes that can see right into your heart. Or settle on your shoulder with their tail curled around, warming your neck, and their hot breath tickling your ear.

Nope, none of these are things you can expect from a cucumber. Well, not any cucumbers I've ever come across. Maybe a mutant radioactive space cucumber, but not your average garden variety. But dragons? Well, they're a whole other story.

So, who wants to grow dragons? Dumb question, right? I mean seriously, who in their right mind would say no? Not me, that's for sure. And not you by the looks of it.

But *if* you want to grow dragons, you need to know what you're getting into. Sure, they're fiery, fantastical, and dazzling, but dragons are not all fun and games. Not by a long shot. And it's not just the fire and the flammable poop I'm talking about. Oh, no!

Which is why, my dragon-seeking desperados, I'm writing this all down, so at least you can go into it with your eyes open. Because, believe me, you'll need them to stay wide, *wide* open.

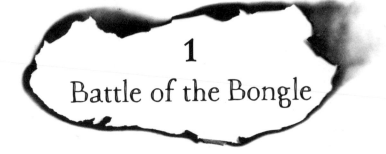

1
Battle of the Bongle

It started about a year ago. And it was all Grandad's fault. Well, his and the jelly doughnut's. I was just licking the last of it off my fingers when he said:

"We should grow our own, Chipstick."

"Doughnuts?" I asked.

"Raspberries." He grinned. "Then we could make our own jelly for Nana's doughnuts. We could mix them up, too. Strawberry and blackberry, gooseberry and raspberry—just think of the possibilities. *Deeeelicious!*"

It did make a pretty good picture in my head, a

vast plate-sized jelly doughnut with different-colored sections like a multi-topping pizza.

"And more, too," Grandad went on, before I could dive further into the jelly dream. "Radishes, beans, onions, cauliflowers . . . You name it, we could grow it."

Suddenly I wasn't so sure it was a great idea. Strawberry and cauliflower jelly? *Ew!* Anyway, I had enough fruit and vegetables to deal with, what with Mom shoveling in my five servings a day. I mean, she even sneaked dried fruit into perfectly good flapjacks— as if I wouldn't notice!

But Grandad wasn't one to let go of an idea once it had fluttered down and settled. So on Saturday morning, there we were at the end of his garden, up to our ears in mud, digging away at what looked to me like a monster jungle. In fact, I was beginning to realize why Mom had offered me provisions for my "trip to the Amazon." Without the nettles and brambles, my grandparents' garden was probably half as big and it still ran all the way down to the fields and beyond.

"I've been wanting to dig into this since we moved in," Grandad told me, pausing to catch his breath, "but what with one thing or another, I just haven't found the time."

I stopped digging and scraped my shovel across a chunk of mud. I know *you* have no idea what he was talking about, but I did. I knew *exactly* what he meant by "one thing or another."

"Sorry," I muttered. Because I really was.

He rested his arms on his shovel and leaned towards me. Now, there's something you should know about my grandad—he twinkles. That might sound weird, but he does. There's a phrase "to have a twinkle in your eye," which means to be bright or sparkling with delight. Well, my grandad has the biggest twinkle of anyone I've ever known. And right then he was shining that twinkle down on me, till I felt its warmth flooding every bit of my body. It was like I'd sat down in front of the toastiest marshmallow-toasting fire.

"Now then, Chipstick, how many times have I told you? What's the deal with families?"

I smiled. "They stick together."

"Exactly." He grinned. "Not unlike jelly doughnuts. Now get digging!"

So I did. The worst thing to dig up was this stuff Grandad called bongleweed—it wound itself around everything, clinging to roots, shoots, and shrubs for dear life.

Soon enough I was in an almighty tug-of-war: boy against plant. And for a moment there, it really looked as if the evil Bongle-Plant Overlord might win.

But I dug. And scraped. And pulled. And heaved. Until all that was left was a patch of earth . . . and the strangest-looking plant I'd ever seen.

It was taller than me, and my blistered hands would have only made it halfway around the trunk. Except it was hard to see the trunk, because of all these long green cactus arms that draped down.

"It looks like a giant upturned mophead," declared Grandad. "But you know—green and spiky and knobbly, too."

Bizarrely, he wasn't far off.

Sprouting from some of the cactus arms were vivid yellow and orange tendrils like bursts of flames. And on each one of those nestled a fruit. Some were large and red and looked like they were about to burst, others were small and green and looked new. But all of them had weird spiky pineapple-like leaves. They were so unlike anything I'd ever seen in our fruit bowl at home. I found myself reaching up to touch them.

I noticed one of the smaller fruits had already turned red, but the tendril it was attached to was being pushed down by the weight of a few larger fruits hanging above. I gently lifted it and moved it to

one side to give it some space. And as I did, I saw something even weirder.

"Hey, Grandad," I called, "it's glowing. Like those fireflies, do you remember? Dad said it was bioloonynonsense or something. He said some jellyfish do it, too."

"Bioluminescence," Grandad corrected. He peered at the red fruit and rubbed a finger across it. "I bet it's just mold," he said. "Come on, Chipstick. I'm famished."

"But what is it?" I asked.

Grandad wrinkled his nose. "No idea, but we can pull it off tomorrow."

I looked at the red spiky fruit that was glowing in my hands. And whether I pulled it a little too hard, or it just chose that moment to fully ripen, one way or another, the fruit dropped from the vivid tendril. Looking at it in my palm, somehow I didn't feel like throwing it into the bonfire pile. So I tucked it under my arm before following Grandad inside.

Later, when I got home, I put the pineapple-y sprouting fruit on my desk and typed "strange spiky fruit" into the search engine on my computer. Pictures popped up and there it was, right next to "durian"—which smell like poop apparently, so it was dead lucky we didn't find those! No, here it was: size of a mango, red, spiky, pineapple-like leaves. Definitely what I had sitting in front of me. I clicked on the picture and read the caption.

Pitaya—"Dragon Fruit"

Yup!

Now, it's easy for *you*. Because you *know* there's

about to be a dragon. But I was clueless back then. I mean, if someone gives you a fairy cake, you don't expect Tinker Bell to pop out, do you?

So I didn't jump up and down screaming, "Whoopee, I'm getting a dragon!" I just left it on the desk and went downstairs for dinner.

And that probably wasn't the best idea. You know, because of what happened next.

2
The Jelly Roll
of Doom

"Is Grandad planning on growing potatoes on your head?" Mom asked when I walked into the kitchen.

She pointed to my hair.

"You've got half the garden in there. Shower, now. And be quick—dinner's nearly done."

I groaned. But there was no point arguing. Not when Mom had her "I will not be moved even by a runaway rhinoceros" look.

But I didn't make it to the shower. And not just because I spotted the latest Spider-Man comic I'd left at the top of the stairs—and stopped to check I hadn't missed anything the six times I'd already read it—but because when I went into my room to grab my robe, I noticed something very odd.

The dragon fruit was glowing. Actually glowing! I went over and peered down at it. Reaching out, I prodded the spiky skin. It started pulsing orange, red, and blazing yellow. And then I remembered what Grandad had said about mold. Maybe it was toxic? I yanked my hand back and stared at it, half expecting

my fingers to shrivel up and drop off in some fatal reaction. They didn't. And the relief was slightly sprinkled with disappointment. Not because I *wanted* my fingers to fall off, but because when you've read as many comics as me, you can't help but hope that you might just absorb some superpowers when this kind of thing happens. Not that this kind of thing *had* happened to me—ever.

The fruit stopped pulsing and now looked pretty normal, apart from the glow. Before I could prod it again, I heard Mom shouting that dinner was ready and if no one was there to eat it in exactly thirty seconds she was giving it all to our next-door neighbor's dog and we could have cereal for all she cared. I might have taken more notice of this if the neighbors actually *had* a dog—which they don't. Just a ferret. And a fussy one at that. So I doubt it'd eat Mom's lasagna anyway.

Dad stuck his head around my door and shouted, "Dinner's ready, Tomas." Then he headed off down the hall.

I waved. "I'm coming, Dad." I didn't bother telling him he didn't need to shout. He wouldn't hear me. He wears a pair of massive headphones pretty much permanently. Music is Dad's job, and his hobby, and what he does in every second between those times, too. He writes music for commercials on TV (and one very low-budget film that no one's heard of, let alone seen), but I think secretly he still wants to be a rock star and imagines being discovered by some TV talent show or something. Anyway, I've gotten used to communicating with him mainly through mime.

Aware that I hadn't made it anywhere near the shower, I swapped hoodies, then ducked into the bathroom and quickly stuck my head under the faucet. Looking at the state of the sink after I'd finished, we'd probably be growing potatoes in there, too!

Mealtimes are interesting in our house. Not because we talk about interesting things or anything like that, but because of my not-yet-three-year-old sister, Lolli. In particular, watching my parents trying

to field the flying food and make sure some of it at least goes into Lolli's mouth.

Plus, since it's the only time Dad doesn't wear headphones and isn't plugged into his keyboards, Mom seems to feel she has to make the most of it by talking nonstop at about a hundred miles an hour. No one could possibly process the amount of information she churns out in between mouthfuls. In fact, I'm pretty sure Dad is actually composing tunes in his head while she's talking, and the nodding Mom takes for his agreement is just him keeping time.

After Mom wiped up the lasagna that Lolli had generously shared with the floor, she brought out dessert. She's working her way through a cookbook Nana gave her last Christmas. That night it was jelly roll and custard. Well, lumps of custard.

"The roll's a bit flat," she noted as she offered it up to us apologetically. "It's supposed to be a nice spiral of dough and jelly. You know, rather than a splodge."

She was right. It looked as if someone had sat on

it. And that wasn't unusual.

Mom is a vet, you see, and although she can wrestle an uncooperative Doberman into a head cone, she can't seem to wrestle ingredients into anything that resembles cake. Despite all the shows she watches on TV.

Of course, that could've had something to do with her leaving out half the ingredients to make it healthier. Sugar-free cake is not cake in my book. But being bombarded with shows about producing the perfect dessert, while at the same time being programmed to make sure everyone eats their five servings of fruit and veggies, makes desserts more difficult for Mom than for the rest of us.

I wanted to say something nice to make her feel better, but I'm really not great at lying. Dad was staring out the window humming under his breath. I needed him to step in quick before I blurted out something that'd probably end up making Mom hurl the whole dish at the wall. Which was not necessarily a bad idea.

Just then Lolli grabbed a piece and stuffed it into her mouth. And then spat it out. Mom looked horrified. We watched as Lolli picked up another piece, unraveled the dough, and happily started licking the jelly out of the middle.

"See? Lolli likes it," I spluttered.

Mom didn't look convinced, so I dived for a piece and started making what I hoped were believable yummy noises.

Mom sighed and just said, "Can't you call her Charlotte for once?"

"But she likes being called Lollibob—don't you, Lollibob Bobalob?" I replied, still chewing a tasteless lump of dough.

Lolli giggled and stuck out two jelly-covered hands to me.

"See?" I said, finally managing to swallow the leaden ball of dessert. It lodged in my throat and I had to take an enormous gulp of water to get it down.

Mom turned and, while she was wiping Lolli clean, I grabbed the rest of the jelly roll from my bowl and stuffed it in my hoodie pocket. Thanks to my sister, I was going to be saved from eating any more. We stick together, me and Lolli. Even without jelly.

Suddenly there was a loud *THUMP!* from upstairs.

Mom stared at the ceiling. "What was that?"

"It's probably just Tomtom messing with my stuff," I said.

"That cat is like a furry wrecking ball," Mom moaned. "Go and sort out your pet, Tomas."

I didn't need to be told twice, not with half a jelly roll still sitting on the table staring at me menacingly. I raced upstairs.

"Tomtom, come out," I said, annoyed as I stepped into my room.

I looked around for the ginger cat, ready to give him his marching orders, but he wasn't anywhere to be seen.

Then I noticed the dragon fruit wasn't where I'd left it on the desk. It was on the floor by my bed. And what's more, it had grown.

3
Is It a Bird? Is It a Plane? Is It Super-Maggot?

So now the dragon fruit was glowing *and* growing.

I decided it was best to keep it out of sight of Mom and Dad and away from Tomtom, so I pulled out one of the storage drawers from the wooden unit that was crammed with all my toys. Shoving a heap of little plastic action figures to either side, I placed the fruit inside. My hands were now covered in sticky goo, like it was oozing juice—or slime.

Remembering the possibility of toxic meltdown, I quickly wiped my hands on my pants. Then I crawled into bed, eyes fixed on the drawer and the glow coming from inside. To be honest, it wasn't the behavior I'd come to expect from fruit. I mean, bananas and mangoes never did this sort of thing. Even with kiwi fruit, you knew where you were. But this? Frankly, it was weird.

I had every intention of keeping a close watch on the fruit but, after all the digging and wrestling with the bongleweed, I was so tired, my nighttime vigil probably lasted about three and a half minutes.

I don't know how long I'd been asleep when my eyes suddenly snapped open. The room was dark, but there was still a glow coming from the drawer. Suddenly the whole wooden unit began to rattle and shake—that must have been what woke me—and then just as quickly, it stopped.

I peeled back the covers and crept out of bed. I switched on my lamp and crouched down next to the drawer. Slowly, I opened it and peered in. The fruit sat there, glowing but unmoving. Had I been imagining

things? I rolled my eyes at my own crazy imagination. And then checked the room for the unicycling gorilla who usually turns up in my dreams. But there was no gorilla. Which meant this was no dream.

I turned back to the fruit and then jumped in alarm as it began to move, shaking the drawer again—and this time I clearly saw one side of it bulge. It was as if something inside was trying to burst out! The skin stretched and the spiky leaves stuck out as the bulge moved under the surface. I thought of the worm I'd once found in a pear from Grandad's garden. What if some kind of monstrous maggot was squirming its way out of the dragon fruit? The thing twisted and writhed and pushed. I started to back away. There was no way I wanted a mutant maggot launching at my face.

But as I took another step, I stumbled over King Kong and came crashing to the floor. I kept my eyes fixed on the still-rattling drawer. And then there was an almighty . . .

POP!

Like a cork from a bottle, something shot over my head. A spray of messy pulp and little black seeds covered the floor and splattered my pant leg. For a second I just lay there, eyes pinned wide open.

Then I heard scratching, and a noise like someone striking a match. I spun around, eyes scanning the floor to see where the maggot—or whatever it was—had landed. But all I could see were the toys I hadn't put away. There was the scratching sound again, like the fizzle of a match igniting. Whatever was making the sound was behind my beanbag. The match struck for a third time.

I edged closer, keeping my eyes firmly on the mound of the beanbag. As I bent towards it, one edge moved. There was something wriggling underneath, trying to squirm its way out. Where was Tomtom when I needed him? He'd left enough sad little critters on my carpet over the years as "presents"—he'd definitely know what to do with some kind of mutant fizzing worm. My heart was hammering in my chest. I'd have run a mile, but if I took my eyes off it, it might slink away and then I'd have to go back to bed knowing it could be somewhere in the room with me.

I grabbed a mug from the desk and stood up, ready to trap whatever it was.

Slowly and very, very gingerly, I lifted a corner

of the beanbag. Every bit of me was poised, ready to jump out of my skin if the thing came shooting out at me. I lifted the beanbag higher, inch by inch, until I saw it, lying curled underneath. The mad hammering in my chest started to calm as I gazed down at the tiny creature in front of me, which was most definitely not a mutant maggot. Although what it was I had no idea.

It looked like a bird. But it had thorny little spines down its back and it seemed more leathery than feathery. It was bright red and its wings were scalloped, a bit like a bat's. And it shimmered in the light of my lamp, like it was having trouble deciding on the very best shade of red to be.

As I stood there, my mouth gaping, it raised its head, swung it from side to side, and sneezed. Only what came out wasn't spit and boogers, but a bright little spark and a wheeze of smoke. And that's when my brain woke up and I knew—for sure and no messing—that what was nestled in my Batman robe, scratching its claws across Robin's head as it hopped from foot to foot, was an actual dragon!

4
IT'S A DRAGON!

OK, so maybe you'd be totally cool if you found a dragon in your bedroom. Maybe it wouldn't phase you at all, and you'd know just what to do. You'd be all like, "Hey, cool, that's a cool dragon. I'm cool about that." But me, I didn't have a clue about what to do and I definitely wasn't feeling cool about it. I mean— it *was* a dragon. It might only have been big enough that it could sit on my hand and so far its fire-breathing had only produced a spark, but hello, IT WAS A DRAGON!

It made the strange fizzling-match sound again.

And the most I could manage to get out at this point was a whispered "Whoa."

Then we stared at each other. For a really long time.

My head is always brimming with ideas and stories. Miss Logan says my imagination is like a geyser gushing out ideas twenty-four hours a day. But right then, it was like the geyser had been sat on by one of those enormous elephant seals with the weird shrunken trunk and all I could squeeze out was:

There's a dragon . . .

in my room . . .

on my carpet . . .

right . . .

now.

Talk about stating the obvious! Then, bit by bit, the elephant seal flubbered away and the geyser spluttered back to life. I pictured my dragon shooting out mighty flames and me riding across the sky on its back. And I thought,

I'M GOING TO HAVE THE MOST UTTERLY, MIND-BLOWINGLY, AMAZINGEST PET OF ALL TIME. (Move over, Liam "I have the best bike/scooter/radio-controlled biplane and obstacle-leaping hamster" Sawston, and make room for my DRAGON!)

Suddenly the little creature took a flutter-hop towards me. And for a second, I wondered if it would turn out to be as mean as all the books said and launch itself at my face. Maybe it'd shoot flames at my eyes. Or scratch me with its sharp claws. This could be a DANGEROUS pet.

I'd probably go into school with scars and have to explain how I'd had to wrestle my pet to the ground before I could get out the door. I guess that might not be ideal. Not on a day-to-day basis anyway. I started weighing the pros and cons, remembering the cuddly class guinea pig, then comparing it to a ferocious, limb-shredding, fire-breathing reptile. But even with the possible loss of limbs, there didn't seem much of a contest: A dragon would make a really cool pet. And the more I watched it, the more I realized that this particular dragon didn't look very mean or dangerous. In fact, as it tilted its head to one side and hiccupped out a little smoke ring, the word that kept popping into my head was "cute."

I stayed as still as I could. I remembered something about letting dogs sniff your hand before you say hello to them, so when it didn't move again, I slowly reached out my hand, resting it on the carpet just in front of the little creature. Another flutter-hop and there was a dragon sitting on the palm of my hand. An actual live dragon!

It kept its wings half unfurled as it swept its head from side to side, inspecting my fingers, which were now warm from its breath. I could feel its claws treading into my skin like a cat trying to get comfy. I didn't dare move in case it disappeared in a puff of "this can't really be happening" smoke.

Slowly I got to my feet, keeping my hand as steady as I could. Suddenly he—I decided to assume it was a he—started jiggling from foot to foot, leaning forward as if he was about to launch and then pulling back. Like I did on the diving board at the pool, wanting to dive but hating the moment when I'd have to step off into nothing but air. I thought about how baby birds learn to fly, and also how I'd seen their tiny bodies on the ground sometimes. The ones who had flown too soon. Was it the same with dragons?

Before I could open my mouth to speak, he had taken the plunge. For a moment, the tiny dragon was flapping upward, nose thrust forward, his wings shimmering. But then he blew out a smoky puff and began to drop, and my heart sank. I lurched forward to catch him, but just before he landed in my outstretched hands, he flapped and rose again. And he was off, soaring away over my bed. Still reeling a bit from side to side, but most definitely aloft. I watched as he swooped back around and landed with a bump on my desk. In my relief and excitement—because let's be clear, a dragon had just flown around my bedroom!—I clapped my hands and gave a whoop of delight. The little dragon lifted his head. He let out another smoky hiccup, this time followed by a tiny orange spark and then he hopped towards me.

Things I noticed from close up:
Glittery wings
Scales that rippled through every shade of red
Eyes like diamonds
Hot, smoky breath
Sharp claws (three at the front, one at the back of
    each foot)
Arrowhead tail (which he didn't seem to be able to
    control very well, because every so often, he
    would whip it around and bash himself, and
    then twist his head around in alarm as if he was
    being attacked)
Two little horns—one longer than the other

Things I did *not* notice: Tomtom

5
The Tomtom
and Jerry Show

Tomtom is big for a cat. In fact, he's gargantuan. I'm pretty sure he's half tiger. And he's on the grumpy side. He's not a cuddly, sit-on-your-lap-and-have-a-lovely-pet kind of cat. He's more of a guard cat.

And I'd left the door open.

So, if you've ever seen Tom and Jerry cartoons—especially the ones with that little yellow canary—you can probably picture what happened next. But if not, then here's what I saw:

My tiger-shaped cat leaping from the bed in a slow-motion arc.

My new dragon in Mad Panic Mode launching into the air, leaving a trail of scorch marks across the walls, his scales flaring a bright electric orange.

Tomtom—who had obviously forgotten he was wingless and unable to fly—very quickly came crashing down on my desk. He sent my lamp, books, and pens flying as he skittered across and landed in an undignified

heap right on top of my remote-control car.

Apparently not finished in his starring role in the new Tomtom and Jerry show, the cat's claws hit the big red button on my remote. This fired up the shrieking siren and spinning lights, which sent him rocketing under my bed with an earsplitting yowl.

I stared at the door. There was no way my parents

would sleep through this racket, and I wasn't sure Lolli would either. The little dragon flew upwards and crashed into my lampshade. His claws ripped through the paper of the shade as he scrambled to hang on to the wire frame. For a moment he swung there upside down, not quite knowing what to do, before heading for the shelf where all my Lego models were lined up. He knocked his way past model after model and I watched in horror as hours of painstaking building tumbled to the ground.

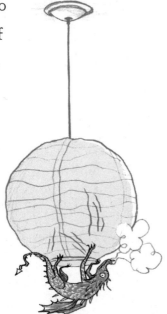

CRRRAAASH...

BANG!

I lunged just as Mom started to enter the room. I poked my head out, trying not to let my eyes drift over to the little dragon perched on the shelf just behind the door.

"What on earth is going on?!" she hissed. Her eyes flicked to Lolli's door.

Dad appeared behind her, looking like his hair had exploded on the top of his head and brandishing a slipper as though he thought we were being attacked. Although what help a pink fluffy slipper would be, I had no idea.

"Sorry," I spluttered. "Tomtom was attacking my King Kong. I had to save it."

Mom frowned. I could tell she wasn't convinced. She tried to peer past me to see inside, but I wedged my foot against the door.

"What's that smell?" she asked, wrinkling her nose.

I sniffed. And caught the faint smoky tang in the air. As if on cue, the little dragon sent out another spark that crackled in the darkness of the room.

"Nothing," I stammered. "Just you know, stinky cat smell. I'll give Tomtom a bath tomorrow, I promise."

Mom looked about to speak, but thankfully a well-timed scream from a grumpy-at-being-woken Lolli sent her attention away from me and the dragon who had just launched up to the lampshade. She groaned and steered Dad down the hall. They disappeared into Lolli's room, Dad still clutching the slipper.

Behind me, Tomtom hadn't given up. With eyes full of malice, he stalked back and forth, getting ready to pounce again. The little dragon was swooping and diving in dizzying circles now, clearly terrified. He kept sending out flurries of little sparks that rained down but thankfully fizzled out before they landed.

I glared at Tomtom. "Out," I hissed, and herded the spitting ball of fury onto the landing.

As soon as the door closed, the dragon flew down towards me and I held out my arm for him to perch on. He was shaking, and as he pulled in his wings, I gently laid my hand across his back.

His eyes were still fixed on the door as if he thought Tomtom might come crashing back through it any second. And I held my breath until I heard Mom and Dad stumble back to their room.

The little dragon's claws dug into my arm as if he was ready to spring at a moment's notice. I couldn't exactly stroke him like you would a cat—well, any cat other than Tomtom—but I kept my hand resting there until he'd stopped shivering and relaxed his grip.

"Sorry," I whispered. "We'll be more careful from now on."

He stared up at me, his twinkling eyes looking right into me. It was like gazing into one of those crystal prisms, where the light is scattered into a rainbow. Fragments of color sparkled and danced around the dragon's almond-shaped irises. I could have looked into those eyes forever. Then, just for a second, his sharp little claws tightened on my arm again.

"I promise," I whispered.

The grip loosened; the tiny creature seemed satisfied that he'd made his point. His scales flickered and the fiery orange glow gradually returned to ruby red.

It was only then that I took in the devastation that was my room. The scorch marks up the walls and the sparks that had left sizeable black stains on the carpet. And the poop. I learned my first important lesson about baby dragons that night. They poop *a lot*. Especially when they're being attacked by a miniature tiger!

6
Banana Blobalob

When I woke up next morning, the first thing I did was swing my head over the edge of the bed and look underneath. And there he was. My dragon. Curled

up in the shoebox nest I'd fashioned for him, the toilet paper expertly shredded into a cozy bed. His bright eyes were fixed on mine, his shimmering red body glowing like a hot ember.

Yup, I had a dragon! I didn't need a groomable guinea pig or a dog who could dance, or even a camouflaged lionfish. Nope. I had a *dragon*. Beat that, Liam!

And OK, I admit he was small. You might even say tiny—something I knew all about, being the smallest in my class—but it didn't seem to be bothering him. Maybe if I glowed like that and could fly, it wouldn't bother me so much either.

I wondered how fast he'd grow and suddenly thought of Lolli. She'd be a bite-size snack for a

growing dragon! As if to reassure me, the little dragon hopped towards my Swiss cheese plant—which isn't actually made of cheese, though how cool would that be for late-night snacks?—and started tearing chunks off it.

"Phew." I laughed. "Well, at

least that's one thing I know now. You eat

plants. Let's just hope I can fill you up with

enough of those."

The only question really was how was I going to keep him? Because I was pretty sure a dragon was not on Mom's list of ideal houseguests. In fact, although my mom and dad put up with quite a lot, looking around at the devastation in my room, I thought even they'd object to *this*.

I'd already had to hide Dad's old Batman comic— well, the sad, charred remains of it. And seven of my socks, singed to smithereens after I'd used them as mittens to put out sparks. And then of course there was the huge hole in Mom's best towel. Oh, and the endless ticking time-bomb poop grenades that lurked here, there, and everywhere. You see, apart from smelling like rotten fish wrapped in stinky cheese with sprinklings of burned toast, dried-out dragon poop is *highly* combustible. Which means that it can explode

without warning. Something I had found out at about four o'clock in the morning. Let's just say that once you've woken up to find your bed splattered with detonated dragon droppings, you get really particular about cleaning them up. And keeping a close eye on where they land!

At breakfast I sat next to Lolli, with my dragon tucked away in my hoodie pocket. I could hear Mom and Dad upstairs, both reeling out their lists of "To Dos."

It was beginning to sound like a competition of whose list was longest. I just hoped none of those "To Dos" ended up coming my way!

Now Lolli may only be little, but she's not dumb. She sees stuff. If I've got a candy in my mouth—even if I'm not chewing—she still knows. And her hand goes out quick as a flash demanding one, too. So when I kept absentmindedly fiddling with my pocket, I think she thought I had some candy hidden in there. She leaned over and pulled at my hoodie, stretching the pocket open.

"Lollwanlollwanlollwan," she gabbled.

Before I could stop him, the dragon saw his chance for freedom and shot out. But in his excitement, he managed to sneeze and poop at the same time. Shooting out fiery sparks from one end that scorched Lolli's toast, and leaving a squelchy mess from the other all over my cornflakes.

Alarmed by Lolli's shrieks of delight, he soared up to the ceiling light, dropping more well-timed poop bombs along the way. One of which perfectly met the sole of Dad's shoe as he strode into the kitchen. If my dad had picked up any tips at our one and only ice-skating lesson, he might have been fine. And if the table hadn't been there he might have slid smoothly through and out the back door. But as it happened, he sort of folded over it as he folds over the table like a crocodile's mouth shutting and landed with his face in Lolli's plate of mashed banana.

At least Lolli thought it was funny.

I quickly opened my pocket and the dragon zipped back in out of sight. Just in time too, as Mom came running in to see what all the noise was about.

"What on earth is going on now?" she groaned, seeing the mess.

Now the good thing about Lolli is that because she can't talk much yet, you can blame quite a lot on her— and the best bit is she finds everything so funny she doesn't even mind and Mom and Dad don't get cross with her because she's only little.

"Lollibob was painting another banana picture and this pigeon flew in and ate it," I said.

Lolli flapped her arms, launching another blob of banana that delicately splatted on Dad's nose and made her squeal again. Mom raised her eyes and sighed. Lolli giggled and stuck her two thumbs up, both covered in banana.

"Lolli blobalob," I said, laughing.

She wiggled her banana-y fingers about like little puppets—which was pretty hysterical and even Mom couldn't help smiling. I told you we stick together, me and Lolli.

Anyway, while Mom acted like a hyperactive octopus, mopping up Dad, the floor, and Lolli, I was able to escape. Which was just as well because I needed to get back to Grandad's garden—fast.

7
Doughnuts and Dragon Fruit Crumble

My grandparents only live a couple of streets away and I can cut through the park to get to their place. In fact, if the new houses at the bottom of our road hadn't been built, I'd be able to see their house from my bedroom window.

The reason they live so close is because when I was younger, I had a hole in my heart. Which sounds pretty weird, I know. I mean, what does that even look like? I always imagined being able to stare through it like my heart was a doughnut. But it wasn't actually like that. I mean, for one thing there wasn't pink icing and hundreds and thousands of sprinkles lining my insides like on a doughnut, which would at least have made up for stuff a bit. But I was pretty sick when I was little and so Nana and Grandad moved here to help look after me while Mom and Dad were at work.

When I was about five, I had to have an operation because the doughnut hole wasn't closing up like they'd hoped. When I heard the word "operation," I thought it would be like that game where you have to fish things out with tweezers. And I couldn't stop worrying that I'd make this horrible buzzing noise and startle the doctor so much he'd fling my heart across the room. But he reassured me that he'd played that game for years and never been buzzed, not once, so I let him do the operation, for real. And he did a good job.

But Mom and Dad still won't accept that it's fixed now and I'm better. They still think I'm fragile and would like to put me in one of those giant plastic bubbles you can bounce around in at fairs, to keep me safe. It's a good thing Grandad's here; he's a firm believer in "letting kids be kids."

He says I need to be allowed to find stuff out for myself. Even if sometimes that means I get a few bumps and scrapes.

Like the time I showed him my design for roller skates after Mom and Dad refused to get me some. It involved a lot of glue, tape, and ballpoint pens. But he let me build them anyway. It wasn't a total success, but I *did* learn how much the floor hurts when you hit it with your face. Which is in itself an important lesson, Grandad said.

So, like I say, I'm totally fine now. Apart from being a teeny bit on the teeny side—and the doctor said I'll probably shoot up like a bean one day. But I'm still waiting for that.

On the upside, it means Nana and Grandad live only two minutes and forty-five seconds away. On the downside, I can't help wondering if all that looking after me was what made Grandad sick. Because now

he has a funny heart, and not the funny-ha-ha kind. Mom and Dad insist it has nothing to do with me, and Nana says it's more likely because of all the bacon and cheese he used to eat, but I still can't help thinking Grandad was supposed to be retired and taking it easy, not running around after me. I wasn't a patient patient. I didn't like being sick, and sometimes when I watched my friends all playing soccer and I wasn't allowed, I used to get really angry. I even remember shouting at Grandad and hiding from him on purpose—so he had to look for me for ages. Which can't have been very nice—or restful.

But whenever I start to worry about him, he accuses me of sticking *him* in a giant plastic bubble. So even though there'll always be this little raw bit deep down in my belly whenever I think of that, I keep it to myself.

When I arrived that morning, I headed straight around the back. I could see Nana through the kitchen window, leaning over a huge saucepan, steam swirling up around her. A sweet, fruity smell came floating out towards me.

I gave her a wave and hurried down to the garden, across the neat lawn, through the little group of apple and pear trees with their low, crooked branches, and on past the abandoned beehives, which Grandad is always promising to clean up but never has.

And then I saw him in the far corner, shovel poised, ready to tear up the roots of the dragon fruit tree. I shrieked and ran towards him.

"Grandad, stop!"

"Hey, Chipstick. Hope you've brought your muscles," he said. "We need to move this thing. Then we can start planning what's going where."

He pointed his shovel at the dangly cactus-like tentacles.

"But, Grandad," I panted, trying to catch my breath, "I found out what it is. It's a dragon fruit tree."

I quickly stepped in front of his outstretched shovel. "I looked it up last night."

Grandad's face wrinkled. "Never heard of one of those."

He angled the shovel again, ready to go to battle.

"I thought I could look after it," I spluttered.

"But it's taking up half the veggie plot. We could get some nice beans in there. Wouldn't you prefer some nice beans?"

I shook my head till I thought my brains would fall out, then blurted out the only thing I could think of that might make him change his mind. "Didn't you want some fancy fruit? Think of it: dragon fruit jelly. You don't get many dragon fruit jelly doughnuts, do you?"

Grandad rested on his shovel and peered across at me. He was giving me his "What are you up to?" look. Then he winked and said, "Best tell Nana to prepare for some dragon fruit crumble as well then, don't you think?"

He turned away and began battling with a bramble. I breathed a sigh of relief. Pulling open my pocket, I stared down at the little dragon curled inside. His bright diamond eyes twinkled back up at me.

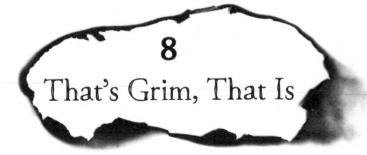

8
That's Grim, That Is

For the next hour, Grandad had me hard at work. I'd left my hoodie, with the little dragon in the pocket, on a pile of dry grass cuttings. He'd seemed happy enough to stay curled up since the excitement at breakfast. But I couldn't help casting glances at it and smiling at the thought of what lay inside. I can't say I was all that heroic about the digging we were doing, but every time I started moaning, Grandad popped a caramel toffee in my mouth.

We were just loading another wheelbarrow with tangled brambles when someone grunted. We both turned and saw a grim-looking man in faded blue overalls wielding a garden fork like it was a lethal weapon. He was leaning across the wire fence that separated Grandad's garden from the one next door.

"What'd you think you're playing at?" he said, pointing at me.

"To be fair, I'm not sure he'd say this was playing." Grandad chuckled.

He was right! I had blisters on my blisters from all the digging.

"I've had vandals in my garden, you know," the man said. "Caused all sorts of mess. Kids mucking about in those fields think they can go where they like, including my garden. No respect anymore. I won't be having it. I'll be watching. And I'll be taking matters into my own hands next time it happens." And he pointed a threatening finger at me as if I was the one to blame.

"Well, this here is my grandson and he's doing me a big favor by clearing the garden with me," Grandad said, still friendly but his voice firm. "He's a good kid. He won't need watching."

The man glared at me, like he was waiting for me to show my true colors, and eventually growled, "You just keep away from what's mine, you hear?"

I opened my mouth to speak, but Grandad popped a toffee in so I couldn't get the words out.

Then the man pointed his fork past us towards the ugly heap of debris we'd piled up from our digging. There was lots and lots of bongleweed.

"You'd better not let that lot near *my* garden. Bloody stuff—once it takes a hold, you can never get rid of it. You won't get anything growing in there, not after that weed's dug its roots in."

"Well, it's early days, but we'll get there," said Grandad, ignoring the old man's tone. He was like a chirpy robin cheerfully making its nest on a Rottweiler's head.

"What a disgrace this is," the man said, waving in the general direction of Grandad's garden, and he turned away, mumbling something else under his breath.

"Who *is* that?" I asked.

"That's our new neighbor, moved in a month or so ago. Name's Jim."

"Grim is more like it," I muttered.

We watched him stomp off towards his shed, where he wrestled with the huge padlock. He slammed the door behind him and for a second we saw his face at the window, glowering out at us. Then a piece of ragged curtain was roughly pulled across.

"Poor fella," Grandad said. "Bet he just sat on a bumblebee."

That's something that always amazes me about Grandad. He's brilliant at dealing with people. Even if someone is being horrible, he doesn't let it bother him. Not like it always bothers me. Instead of feeling angry or being rude back, Grandad actually seems to stick up for them. "Poor guy," he'll say, "bet it was his birthday and everyone forgot."

Me, I think some people are just like that. Rude, I mean. What was Grim's problem, pointing his bony finger at me? As if I'd go near his stupid garden.

I was pretty sure it wasn't vandals either—at least not the kind he was thinking of. Because I'd seen something that Grim hadn't.

There were dragon fruits littering the ground around the tree. They had burst open, leaving trails of messy pulp across the dirt. I counted them. One. Two. Three. Four. Five. Six. Six burst fruits.

But did that really mean there were six tiny dragons hatched and on the loose? If so, then where were they now?

As I walked home, I kept my hand in my pocket. I needed to feel the little dragon, just to check that this was all truly happening. Because everyone always says I have a great imagination, and it's true—I don't just daydream, I daydream in Technicolor with surround sound! So it could have all been wishful thinking, couldn't it?

But as I walked, I felt my dragon's claws gently scraping my palm. And then I felt him curl up in my hand, coiling his tail around my wrist. And I knew this was no daydream. This was the real deal.

I looked up at the clouds and imagined my dragon flying through the sky, fully grown. Soaring up into the blue, a jet of flame blazing from his mouth, me on his back . . . Inside my pocket, his hot breath warmed my skin, and with every puff, the dream of flying flared brighter.

But by the time I'd gotten home, I knew that dreams of flying would have to wait. Because, let's face it, my dragon didn't even fill a shoebox. I wasn't going to get far on him. And as for jets of flame, the most he spluttered out were sparks. And that was mainly because he kept sneezing. He seemed to have a cold or be allergic to everything!

As I climbed the stairs, the dragon popped his head out of my pocket and sneezed for the gazillionth time. Covering my hand with the end of my sleeve, I caught the glowing spark before it could singe the carpet. I was going to be a pro baseball player at this rate—I'd have the sharpest reflexes in school.

Safely in my room, I lifted him out and settled him on my desk. He hopped around, inspecting things. I wondered what I was going to call him.

Red? Scorch? Blaze?

I tried them out, calling them to him. They were all good dragon names. But none of them quite fit this little shimmering creature.

Obviously unimpressed by any of the names so far, he flew over to my Swiss cheese plant and started nibbling at the few remaining leaves. When he'd eaten

 his fill, he fluttered up to my shoulder and curled his tail around my neck. His scales glimmered turquoise, gold, and back to ruby red. Like a contented wave of color flickering over his body.

Flicker. I smiled and said the word aloud.

The dragon tilted his head and looked at me.

He uncurled himself, rose up into the air, and sent out another spray of sparks in a glittering arc. And as he did, his scales flickered again, this time in the sunlight that shone through my bedroom window.

I laughed, racing to snuff out each spark. "OK, then. Flicker it is."

9
Poop Patrol, Goldfish, and Ninja Tortoises

Monday mornings involve a lot of running, arm waving, shrieking, and crying—it's one of the days Mom goes to work, and the only day Dad doesn't work from home—so getting me to school, Lolli to daycare, and them to work can be a bit of a challenge. For them anyway. I usually just hang out in my room, avoiding all of the above until it's time for breakfast.

But that was before Flicker. On my first school day since the baby dragon had arrived, I was more panicked than Mom and Dad combined.

My first job was poop patrol. I'd already learned the best way to deal with Flicker's poops was with a pair of oven mitts and a water gun. Just in case any had dried out to the point of detonation. Then I used one of Lolli's little plastic shovels from last year's vacation at the beach to scoop them up and drop them down the toilet. Quick wash of the shovel in the sink and the worst job was done.

The next thing was emptying out my toy box and lining it with some fresh paper and my old bathrobe. I was planning on leaving Flicker my cheese plant and a bowl of water. On that first night, I'd been so caught up in the whole "I have a dragon" hysteria, I'd forgotten he'd need to drink. It was only when I'd gone to the bathroom and turned around to see him about to nose-dive into the toilet that I figured that one out. Luckily I caught him just in time. The last thing I wanted was him thinking *that* was the water bowl!

By the time I left for school, I was pretty sure Flicker had everything he'd need to spend the day on his own in my room. But by the time I got to school, I had a nagging feeling I had forgotten something. As I was racking my brain, Ted, Kat, and Kai raced over.

"Hey, Tomas. Did you know humans share fifty percent of their DNA with bananas?" Ted said.

I didn't.

"And they're herbs too, you know."

"Humans?"

"Bananas! They're herbs, not fruit."

I hadn't known that either. But then I wasn't sure anyone other than Ted knew this stuff. His head was full of it.

I've known Ted since we were goldfish. I mean, not actual goldfish, but the size of them. When our moms found out they were pregnant, they went to this class where you find out what to do with babies—I've no idea what they learned, but it had something to do with llamas, I think. That's where they met, and so that's when Ted and I first met—although being squished inside our moms meant our first playdates were a bit limited. We were even due to arrive on the same day—which would have been pretty cool as we'd have the same birthday—but Ted went and barged his way out early, so he had a full two weeks with no best friend, which kind of serves him right.

Kat and Kai we met on our first day of school. They're twins. Like me and Lolli, they genuinely seem to like each other. It doesn't stop them arguing, mind you, but if push comes to shove, if you mess with one, expect the other to come in after them.

So there's the four of us—and it's been like that since forever.

"You OK, Tomas?" Kat asked. "Where'd you get all those scratches?"

I rubbed my arm. Until Flicker had gotten the hang of his tail, every time he batted it around, the arrowhead end had gouged into my skin.

"Er . . . Tomtom," I said hurriedly.

"What about that?" she asked, pointing at my hand.

I fiddled with the plaster. It was just a mild burn from my first poop patrol—before the oven mitt.

"Er . . "

I'm terrible at lying. I panic and then my overactive imagination gets involved. For some reason right then, Nana's tortoise, Jacko, popped into my head. Only he was a ninja tortoise with a jetpack. I was just about to blurt out that I'd been attacked by a torpedo tortoise when luckily I was saved by Mr. Peters ringing the bell.

I lunged for the door, just managing to get in front of Liam "I-rule-the-universe" Sawston.

"Ow!" he wailed. "Sir, Tomas just elbowed me."

I'd actually brushed his arm with the tip of my littlest finger, but Liam's not one to bother with details.

Without hanging around to see if "sir" was going to call me back, I ducked inside and set out for our classroom.

10
Why You Should Never Keep a Dragon in Your Backpack

I'm not known for my brilliant concentration in class. In fact, Miss Logan has repeatedly said she wishes there was an Olympic medal for daydreaming because I'd win gold. By the time I'd absentmindedly glued Amira's sleeve to the table and painted stripes across Seb's left hand, it wasn't just Miss Logan raising her eyebrows. But I couldn't help it. I couldn't stop thinking about what Flicker was doing and if I'd been right to leave him alone at home.

It was then that I noticed Ted's nose wrinkling. He leaned closer. Was he *smelling* me?

I edged away, giving my arm a sniff and scanning my clothes, wondering if I'd gotten so used to the whiff of dragon poop that I hadn't noticed I'd gotten some on me.

"Dude, what is with you today?" Kai whispered. "You're being off-the-scale weird."

But before I had the chance to blame any rogue tortoises, Mr. Firth strode into the classroom.

"Ready for the baseball competition, Miss Logan?" he bellowed. "We've been looking forward to this all semester. I hope you've had your class working on their skills after last semester's basketball fiasco."

Miss Logan smiled serenely.

"I think we're ready for you, Mr. Firth."

"Oh, I doubt that, Miss Logan, but I suppose we must admire your optimism. Of course, my class depends on ability more than wishful thinking. Anyway, the match has been scheduled for 2 p.m. I'll be taking Lightning Class out for a warm-up beforehand. You're welcome to join us, if you don't think we'll scare the competition."

From the look he gave us as he said the word "competition," it was clear he didn't think we qualified as a serious threat. He didn't throw back his head like some dastardly villain and scoff outright, but we all knew Mr. Firth thought his class was going to wipe the floor with us.

And even Miss Logan didn't look quite so serene after he left.

I could tell Ted, Kat, and Kai wanted to really quiz me when we were on our way out of class, so I hung behind, pretending I'd lost my pen under the table. Part of me would have liked to tell them everything, but another part wanted to keep Flicker all to myself. I'd never had anything as cool as Flicker before and I wasn't sure I was ready to share him. Not yet.

But I was beginning to realize that, with my terrible lying skills, keeping him a secret might not be as easy a I'd thought. The exploding poop didn't help either.

It happened while we were changing into our

gym clothes. I lifted out my shorts, and my heart sank. There were dark scorch marks across the back. But it was the smell that everyone else noticed first. One of Flicker's dried-up poops had exploded, covering every inch of the bag.

Liam screwed up his nose. "Ew, miss, something smells." He looked in my direction. "And I think it might be coming from over there."

Everyone turned to look at me.

It was one of those times you wish you had a pop-up black hole in your pocket, ready to swallow you up.

"I think Tomas had an accident, miss," he said, pretending to whisper behind his hand but actually saying it loud enough for the other class to hear. They were two doors away. Liam was just loving this.

I looked to Ted and Kai, but even they were backing away. I stuffed the shorts back inside my bag, cringing.

While the rest of the class bounded out towards the field, I was sent to lost and found to find some

spare clothes. It wouldn't have been so bad if I'd had a different surname, but as it was, it was like handing Liam a free gift. I'll be stuck with "Whiffy Liffy" for the rest of my life.

On Mondays, Grandad picks me up from school. But today when he asked how my day had been, I just shrugged. I couldn't exactly tell him about the dragon-poop incident, and we'd lost so spectacularly in the baseball game I just wanted to forget the whole day.

"I've been thinking about the garden," Grandad said. "We need to work out what's going where. Got to get the right conditions for each plant or they won't thrive. What do you say? Feel like coming over and helping me plan it out?"

"Er . . . can I come tomorrow?" I said, thinking of how I really just wanted to get home to Flicker.

As we walked through the park, Grandad started

telling me about how we were going to mark out the garden into areas. But I was too distracted to really listen. I kept thinking about the burst dragon fruits I'd seen under the tree. Had more dragons really hatched? Could there be six dragons hiding out in our town? It seemed so unlikely. I mean, with the amount of poop my one little dragon was making, if there was a whole pack of them out there, surely the news would be full of explosions and unexplained fires. People noticed stuff like that, didn't they?

The nagging feeling I'd had during classes grew even worse the closer I got to home. I started walking more quickly, my brain going over and over everything I'd done that morning. And then it landed on me like a cosmic cow pie—the thing I *hadn't* done. I grabbed the front-door key from Grandad's hand and ran, my panic rising. Because the one thing I'd forgotten to do was close my bedroom window!

At home, my fingers fumbled with the lock. I raced up the stairs and flung open the door to my bedroom.

When I looked inside, it wasn't the shredded curtain or the dragon poop on my computer that I noticed first. It was Flicker, perched on the windowsill—at the *open* window. For two days, I'd had the coolest pet in the world. Two days. And now I was about to lose him. I stood frozen to the spot.

"Tomas," Grandad called, coming up the stairs, "you OK? Your pants on fire or something?"

He paused halfway up and looked through the banisters towards my door. I quickly pulled it shut behind me.

"Nah, just checking Tomtom hadn't gotten into my room again," I said. But my voice was far too squeaky to sound casual.

He looked like he was about to quiz me but then said, "Righto. I guess every man's entitled to his secrets—right, Chipstick?" He gave me a wink. "I'm just downstairs if you need me. I'll make us some tea, alright?"

"Yeah. Great. Thanks. Good idea," I said, already

disappearing back into my room.

With the bedroom door safely closed, I turned to face the little dragon. He was still on the windowsill, staring up at the sky, his tail flicking from side to side.

"Flicker," I whispered desperately.

He turned. I reached out a hand towards him, but he launched into the air.

For a heart-stopping moment, I watched him soar up, up, and away. I'd only ever let him fly inside the house. Now, sensing freedom, he was going to simply fly away and leave me. I raced over to the window, my eyes locked on the little shape flitting about among the leaves of the

trees at the end of the garden. After a few agonizing minutes, he fluttered towards the tree in next door's garden, the one nearest my window. He perched on a branch, his diamond eyes fixed on me.

I held my breath to see what he would do next. I waited, my heart ready to crack. Willing him to come back to me. Terrified he wouldn't.

Then, stretching his wings and with his eyes still locked on mine, Flicker flew back in through the window and settled on my shoulder.

And it felt like a firework display was going off inside me.

11
Quiet, Please— No Screaming

I knew if I was going to look after Flicker properly, I needed to know more about dragons and more about the dragon fruit tree. Once Mom and Dad were back and Grandad had left, I sat down at the computer. Just to warn you here, computers and dragon poop *really* don't mix—I'd managed to clean the smelly stuff off before it ignited, but the heat must have fried the keyboard. I grimaced, closed the lid, and headed downstairs to use Dad's work computer.

But I found him staring at a blank screen, muttering things that it was good Lolli wasn't near enough to hear.

"Tomas," Mom called, "I'm just taking Charlotte to the library. We won't be long. Why don't you help your dad while we're gone?"

I looked at Dad's face, scrunched up in fury, and the screwdriver he was waving threateningly at the back of the laptop. And I backed away.

"Actually, Mom, I've got some homework I need to research. The library's just the place I need to be."

When she wasn't standing in our school playground at lunchtime, Mrs. Olive also worked at the town library.

She smiled as I walked in. "Lovely to see you, Tomas. And your little friend, of course."

For a second I thought she meant Flicker and my hand shot to my hoodie pocket, but he was still hidden, curled up and fast asleep. Then I realized Mrs. Olive was smiling at Lolli, who was struggling her way out of the stroller.

I smiled back, relieved.

The town library is tiny, not like the big city library. But you can fill in request forms and get books sent from any of the other libraries in the area.

"Little bit of magic," Mrs. Olive always says. "I can summon your book with one click." I got the feeling Mrs. Olive liked the idea that the world was a little bit magic.

"Me-wan-dagon me-wan-dagon," Lolli gabbed as she tottered in behind, her hands reaching for me.

Mom looked frazzled, which I guess is what walking half a mile with a demanding two-year-old does to you.

"What do you want now, Charlotte?" Mom said, feebly dangling a series of half-chewed toys, a cookie, and a carton of juice in front of her.

Lolli started pulling at my pocket and I tried to push her hands away.

"Mewanna *dagon*," she insisted.

I backed away, aware that both Mom and Mrs. Olive were staring at me now.

"Whatever it is, just give it to her," Mom pleaded, obviously fearing a Lolli meltdown.

If I wasn't careful, this was not going to end well. I bent down to my little sister and whispered in her ear, "Flicker's sleeping."

It was enough to make her let go of my pocket. But I could feel Flicker stirring at all the tugging, and when Lolli saw my pocket wriggle, she announced, "Me sing lullyby peas."

Trying my best to smile sweetly at the adults, I took Lolli's hand and led her down to the far end of the library. Mrs. Olive's husband had made this kid-sized train you could sit in, with carriages full of picture books and cuddly toys. I settled Lolli on a cushion and lifted Flicker out of my pocket. He gave a little shudder and his scales rippled. But he still looked half asleep as he lowered his head and tucked in his wings.

Lolli grinned and clapped her hands. "Lolliby lullyby," she giggled. "Lolly byebye!"

I put the little dragon on her lap and he curled up quite happily. She started humming and flicking through the pages of a book. A little ripple of turquoise flashed along Flicker's body from snout to tail. It was like a contented purr in color. He'd be asleep again in no time. I left them to it. I had research to do.

Sadly there was only one computer, and there was a sign on it saying it was out of order.

Mrs. Olive saw me staring at it.

"Sorry, Tomas, there was a bit of an incident with a carton of juice last story time. I expect you can find what you need in these though." She swept her hand towards the shelves of books and smiled.

I nodded.

It didn't take me long. The mythology section had a whole shelf on dragons. I grabbed an armful of books and headed over to one of the comfy chairs opposite the library desk. Mrs. Olive had roped Mom into helping her sort some new books and I watched as they disappeared into the stockroom.

I gave a quick glance down to the train, where Lolli was babbling away, her hand pointing to the pictures in the book as if she was telling herself—and Flicker—the story.

Then I curled up in the chair and leafed through the first book. It was all about different types of dragons. I never knew there were so many. Every country seemed to have its own particular type. Some were snake-like with no wings, and others had three heads. In some places, they were seen as terrible fire-breathing monsters, while in others they were actually believed to protect people.

My head was so far away in those distant lands that I didn't notice what was happening down the far end of the library. At least, not until the screaming started.

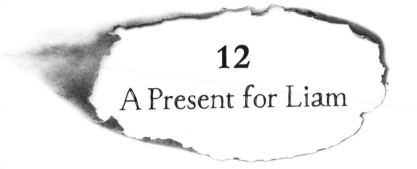

12
A Present for Liam

I recognized the supersonic scream immediately. It was unmistakably Lolli-sized. I leaped up and saw her standing on the train, arms grabbing for the book she'd been looking at. Another child had it clutched to her chest with an equally determined scowl on her face. A lady with a flowery skirt stood between them, trying to make peace.

"Now then, my little peaches, why don't we have a story all together?"

I looked around for Mom and saw her coming out

of the store cupboard with her arms full of books. I could see she was thinking the same as me. A story wasn't going to work with Lolli at this point. And I couldn't say I blamed her. After all, the girl had obviously snatched the book away from her in the first place.

I sprinted down there. The flowery lady was insisting on story time and was just about to take a seat, squashing her flowery bottom into the far-too-small-for-it train. Lolli's next scream smashed the sound barrier. And I suddenly saw why. Among the cuddly toys, I spotted a scaly head with two little horns peeking out. The woman was just about to flatten poor Flicker!

In a heroic moment—or maybe it was just the reflexes of an angry and alarmed two-year-old—Lolli bent over and rammed the lady off the train like a stampeding baby rhino.

There was a screech from the lady as she tumbled forward, and then a crash as the shelf she staggered into went flying. Books scattered across the carpet and the air filled with the cries of Mom and Mrs. Olive as they descended on the book corner to rescue her.

While the adults stumbled around trying to help the woman to her feet, I saw Lolli point at the picture book. As I watched, it rose up into the air and started to fly across the library, banging into shelves and ceiling lights as Flicker, whose wings were making the open pages flap noisily, struggled to find the exit.

The little girl who had grabbed the book stood there watching, her mouth forming a little round O as she tried to make sense of the flip-flop-flapping book above her. And when Lolli pointed a grubby finger at her, she backed away as if she feared she might be next to fly across the room.

Finally Flicker headed straight for the open door. I dashed after the flying book and was just in time to see it smack straight into Liam Sawston's head.

He staggered on the steps and dropped his bike, nursing the lump that was already bulging on his forehead. His eyes shot to the book, which had fallen to the floor. I bet poor Flicker was just as stunned.

"You threw that at my head. I'm gonna get you for that!"

"I-I didn't," I stammered. "Honest."

I could see Liam's anger growing. I wouldn't have been surprised if his T-shirt had split open and shown green muscles rippling underneath. It was definitely an Incredible Hulk moment. And as he hulked up, I seemed to shrink even smaller than usual.

He reached forward to grab the book, presumably to fling it back at me. I glanced down and noticed it wasn't moving. What if Flicker was hurt? Either way, I couldn't let Liam find him. I shut my eyes and imagined myself turning red-hot, like an ember, like a spark about to explode.

And I did what Lolli had done. I became a rhino and charged. The trouble is, with my eyes shut, my maneuver was less successful than Lolli's. Liam just sidestepped and I ended up tripping over his bike and crashing headfirst into a shrub. Luckily for me, he had sidestepped into something sqishy and he landed in an equally undignified heap.

"Whatever's going on?" Mrs. Olive cried, striding towards us.

She bent down, her hand reaching for the book. My arm shot out. "Wait," I cried.

It was too late. She lifted it up as I sat there with leaves and ladybugs in my hair, powerless to stop her.

But Flicker was nowhere to be seen! I think the sigh of relief that came out of me was probably worthy of a hurricane rating. Definitely enough to knock someone's hat off, anyway.

"I hope you haven't been throwing my books around," Mrs. Olive continued. If there was one thing that would turn sweet Mrs. O into your worst nightmare, it was mistreating books. This was something Liam had been known to do so her attention was focused directly on him. Unfair I know, but I wasn't about to start feeling sorry for him.

Liam glared at me, scraping what I realized must be dragon poop off his sneaker, then grabbed his bike and staggered away down the street. As he passed under one of the trees, he yelped and his hand shot to his head. I could just make out a little flitting shape among the leaves. I grinned. It looked like Flicker had dropped a final parting gift on him. The icing on the cake, you might say.

13
Slugs and Superheroes

Mom had already stormed ahead with Lolli, who was strapped into her stroller and happily occupied with a book and a rice cake the size of her head. As I trailed slowly home, I tucked my hand in my pocket and scratched Flicker along the ridges of his back. He rumbled under my hand, contented.

He didn't seem to have grown at all, despite the fact he was eating around thirty-three meals a day. He was always nibbling something. After all the extra broccoli I was sneaking off my plate and getting him to dispose of, he still sat comfortably on my hand. Even so, I couldn't help drifting back into the dream of us flying together. Unfortunately the dream didn't last long.

"Hey, lamebrain."

I stopped in my tracks as Liam raced up on his bike and skidded to a halt in front of me. He planted himself on the pavement, blocking my way.

"I've been watching you, you and those other meebas."

So, I'm guessing by now you're getting a picture of Liam? Big nose for barging into other people's business, stirs up trouble like he's frothing a milkshake, acts like he owns the world.

Well, he also has his own special brand of mean nicknames. Sadly for him, a lot of them don't actually make sense and so aren't as cutting as he'd probably like them to be. Take "meeba," for instance. What I think he's actually going for is "amoeba." An amoeba is a small, single-celled organism without a brain. The fact he thinks it's "a meeba, two meebas" just shows

who's really lacking a brain around here.

"I've seen you," he sneered.

I curled my hand around Flicker, who seemed to have fallen asleep in my pocket. His hot breath sent little shivers of warmth right through me. It felt like even though he was tiny and asleep, he was protecting me.

"Well, that's terrific," I said.

This is the point where Ted might have elbowed me into shutting up. But without him around, and with a dragon in my pocket, I just couldn't help myself.

"I see you, too. A bit old for peekaboo, aren't we?"

You could almost see the steam puffing from Liam's ears when I said it.

"Watch it, ant-boy, or I'll squish you like the insect you are. You know what I'm talking about. You're up to something. First at school, and then at the library. You're being weird, even for you."

"Nope, just the usual amount of weird." I grinned.

He narrowed his eyes and stepped towards me,

leaning close. I suddenly wished Ted's elbow had been there after all. I had a feeling Liam was about to turn nasty.

"Well, I say you're being extra-weird. And I'm going to find out what you're up to."

He reached out and shoved me, and I stumbled into a tree.

"And it'll be easy 'cause I can smell you coming a mile away, Whiffy. You're stinkier than those stink bombs my brother got me last Christmas."

I rubbed my arm, feeling the bruise. And then my heart did that skippy thing like when Dad drives too fast over a speed bump. What if being slammed into the tree had crushed Flicker? My hand automatically reached for my pocket and Liam's eyes followed.

"What have you got in there?" he sneered.

I felt Flicker moving. He was OK! But the relief didn't last, as I felt the little dragon pushing against my hand, trying to get out. I curled my fingers around his body, desperately hoping it might settle him down.

"Nothing. Look, I'm not up to anything," I said quickly. But I could feel my heart beating faster and faster, and my hands were getting sticky with sweat. And it wasn't just from panicking about Flicker being seen; I could feel the dragon heating up, too. He was as unhappy about getting shoved as I was. I couldn't risk him being seen, but the more panicky I felt, the hotter he got. I needed a distraction—and quick!

"Well?" Liam said as he flicked a slug from the top of a wall in my direction. It landed on my jacket, so I carefully placed it in the safety of a nearby bush. Poor

99

little thing. I'm not saying I love slugs, but it had just been minding its own business.

Anything I said at this point was likely to make things worse, but not saying anything wasn't helping either. I could tell Liam was about to go full Hulk. He was getting bigger again, his muscles bulging before my eyes. I waited for the sound of his T-shirt ripping.

But before he could squash me with his great green fists, three people suddenly appeared by my side.

Ted, Kat, and Kai. Materializing there like my own personal superhero squad.

"Hey, Tomas. Need a hand with Liam the Unincredible Hulk?" Kai said.

The relief of having my friends there felt like finally getting a Blizzard from Dairy Queen on the hottest day of the year after joining the Guinness World Records longest ice-cream line.

I imagined the four of us standing in formation in front of him, wielding our superpowers as Kai's words blasted out like lasers, shrinking Liam to the size of a pea. It must have done the trick, because although he kept up the scowl, Liam got on his bike and pedaled off.

"You OK, Tomas?" Ted asked once he'd gone.

"Yeah, thanks. I'm fine." As I said it, I felt Flicker's heat begin to fade, as if he too, was calming down.

"What's up with him?" Kai asked, nodding towards the retreating Liam.

"Has he been hassling you about . . . you know, the PE stuff?" Kat asked.

I bent down and pretended to tie my shoelace, aware of them watching me, and willing Flicker not to try to wriggle out. Or worse, poop. The last thing I needed was another Whiffy Liffy episode. Even my friends thought I was being weird, without that happening. I spotted Mom and Lolli, miles ahead now and just about to turn the corner onto our street, and I willed her to turn around and call me.

"Nah, you know, just usual Liam stuff," I said.

I knew they weren't buying it. That's the thing about friends. Especially ones who know you as well as these three knew me.

"TOMAS!" Mom shouted.

"I'd better go," I said, rolling my eyes and faking a groan.

I ran off, silently thanking Mom for saving me from another lie. But as I left, I couldn't help noticing that Kat was looking a bit hurt.

Once I was safely on our street, I slowed down. Flicker stretched in my pocket. Mom was already wrestling the stroller through the front door and so, after checking there was no one else around, I reached in to lift him out. He unfurled his wings and shook himself, sending a shimmering ripple across his scales. He sneezed and shot out a spray of sparks that I quickly stamped out.

It was a good thing he hadn't gotten out and done that when the others were there. And, more importantly, that Liam hadn't seen him. I *really* didn't like the idea of him spying on me. I'd just have to be super-careful from now on.

14
Crispy Cornflake
Crumb-Fest

All the next day at school, I could feel Liam's eagle eyes watching me. I tried to act normal and thought I was doing a good job, until I saw Ted, Kat, and Kai whispering and exchanging puzzled glances. Maybe I was getting normal wrong—or maybe I was being *too* normal? Was that even a thing? I didn't have the brainpower to work it out. My head was already full of Flicker and wondering what mess I was going to find when I got home at the end of the day.

That afternoon it wasn't just Flicker who'd made a mess, though. I came into the kitchen and found Lolli covered in a crispy cornflake crust.

My feet crunched across a carpet of rice. Mom was sweeping cereal and dried pasta into little mountains. A river of yogurt flowed between them with splashes of ketchup along its banks. Lolli was sitting in the middle of the scene waving a picture at me.

"I only left her for a minute," Mom sighed. "I had hoped we were over the painting-with-food stage."

Lolli pointed to the mess on the paper and beamed.

"Yeah," I said. "Er . . . great work, Lolli."

She frowned, looked at her picture, and turned it the other way up. Then flapped her arms and made a roaring noise.

Now I'm not sure anyone else would have seen what I saw in her "artwork." But then Lolli and I were the only ones who knew there was a dragon living upstairs. Suddenly I could make out the ketchup flames and the scaly pasta wings and the gluey raisin eyes she'd dipped in glitter. She'd made dragons, and lots of them. She waved it at me again and I took it from her.

"Thanks, Lollibob," I whispered. "I'm sure he'll love it."

And he did. After I pinned it to my wall, Flicker curled up in front of the picture and stayed there, rumbling with contentment.

Meanwhile, I cleared up the lurking poops and hid yet another shredded pillowcase. Feeling pleased with my efforts, I ducked downstairs for a drink—where Mom cornered me.

"Grandad's been telling me all about his plans for the garden," she said while scrambling an egg with one hand and dropping counters into Connect 4 with the other.

Lolli loved undoing the catch and watching all the counters clatter out. She slotted the last ones in and then jiggled up and down in anticipation.

"Sounds like the pair of you have taken on a bit of a project," Mom continued.

I remembered us walking home the day before and how I'd promised him I'd go over today. I smiled awkwardly, a pang of guilt squirming inside my tummy. It was easy to get distracted with Flicker around.

"I haven't seen him fired up like this for ages. It's good." Mom glanced up at me for a second. "But don't leave it all to him now, okay?"

I felt myself blush. Had she just read my mind? If she had, I hoped she didn't read any further and figure out I had a dragon in my room! Anyway, she was right—Grandad needed me.

"I'll go now," I said, marveling at her ability to catch the tiny astronaut Lolli had just launched into orbit before he splat-landed in the egg with one hand, while scooping up the scattered Connect 4 counters with the other. I sometimes wonder if my Mom secretly has her own superpowers.

Flicker was only too keen to get out of the house, and he flitted happily from tree to tree as I walked to Nana and Grandad's house. But every so often, if there was no one in sight, he'd zoom down and send out a puff of smoky warm breath to tickle my ear.

When I arrived, Nana met me with a freshly baked chocolate muffin and gave me a thermos of lemonade for us both. I found Grandad down in the garden with a handful of seed packets, a look of pure concentration on his face.

"Hey, Chipstick. I've got a problem. I can't decide on the best kind of beans to try. I'm a green bean man myself, but there's all sorts here—runner beans, scarlet runner, winged, yard-long. I never knew there were so many. It's up to you really. What do you say? Feel like something a bit more fancy?"

His eyes were twinkling and I could see Mom was right about him being fired up about the garden.

"Er . . ." I said. "I'm more of a baked-bean fan."

Grandad chuckled and ruffled my hair.

It should have been difficult to get excited about any type of bean when I knew there was a dragon just feet away. I doubted even magic beans would beat a dragon.

But it was hard not to get caught up in Grandad's enthusiasm. You couldn't help enjoying yourself with him around. And it wasn't just the constant supply of caramel toffees, either.

Flicker had been happily exploring the hedges and eating his fill of greenery. He was careful to keep out of sight, but every so often I had the feeling he was playing a game with Grandad, flitting down behind him and then zipping off again just as he turned around. Eventually I saw the bright shine of his scales dim a little, a sign he was getting tired, and he disappeared among the cactus-like arms of the dragon fruit tree. When he didn't reappear, I breathed a sigh of relief. At least if he was asleep, I didn't have to worry about Grandad spotting him.

After about an hour of digging and planting, and redigging and replanting when Grandad changed his mind, I leaned my shovel against the old shed and rubbed the ache out of my arms.

"You know, I don't think we're going to get much jelly out of that there tree, Tomas," Grandad said, offering me a glug from the thermos. "Nothing left but the skins of the last few fruit. The squirrels must have gotten them. And I've not seen hide nor hair of any more fruit. You sure we shouldn't just pull the old thing out?"

I leaped up and spluttered through a mouthful of lemonade.

"No, we can't! I'm sure there'll be more."

Grandad didn't look convinced, and I could see

him eyeing up how much more space there would be for his exotic beans without it.

I wished I'd found out more about the tree. The books in the library had shown me loads of different types of dragons, but they had all come from eggs, not trees. There was no mention of a dragon fruit tree in any of them.

What if Grandad was right? What if there was no more fruit? I wouldn't be able to stop him pulling it out if one little crop of squirrel snacks was all the tree had to show for itself. He'd want it gone for sure.

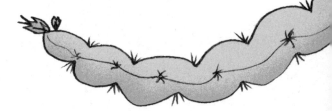

15
Bingo!

"Right, Chipstick, let's see if you're right. Come on."

Grandad pulled open the door to the garden shed and disappeared inside. I followed him, trying not to cough at the dust and the earthy smell. The shed leaned awkwardly and I couldn't help wondering if it might just give up and collapse if either of us so much as sneezed.

On one side there were wooden shelves loaded with empty flowerpots, bits of string, and ancient-looking packets of seeds. Grandad reached up to pull something from the top shelf. It was a huge old book. He swept dust from the leathery cover.

"I spotted this in here the other day when I was rooting around for a trowel. The old woman who lived here before must have left it. She left all sorts of bits and pieces as it happens. But unlike the Guatemalan rain stick, this might actually be useful. It's an encyclopedia of plants."

We laid the book on the little countertop under the window, brushing away as much of the dirt as possible first and sending a family of spiders scurrying to safety.

"*A World of Plants*, it's called," Grandad said. "I was thinking of using it to look up things to grow. Let's see if it's got anything to say about your tree."

The cover was thick with grime, but the lettering of the title was all fancy, like some old spell book you see in films.

I was sure it creaked when we opened it. Inside, the pages were stiff and yellowed, crammed with illustrations and information.

We flicked through, but there was no sign of the strange spiky dragon fruit tree. Until at last Grandad cried, "Bingo!" and thumped his hand down on the counter, half choking me with a dust explosion.

And there it was: the pitaya—our dragon fruit!

I ran my hand over the picture as if I could feel the spiky leaves on the page.

"Looks as if you were right," he said. "Says here we should get five or six crops of fruit at least."

He started reading to me about flowers that bloomed for just one night, but I only had eyes for one thing. In a swirly bordered box at the bottom of the page was a tiny picture of a dragon, and a paragraph of text.

I had found the legend of the dragon fruit! I read the first words, my heart jumping around inside me, eyes skittering over the letters in my excitement.

Sadly, my excitement soon fizzled out. Legend had it that dragons were supposed to breathe out the dragon fruit. But it didn't say anything about dragons

actually growing *inside* the fruit, like Flicker had.

I peered out of the dirt-streaked window, wondering if there really were more dragons out there or if mine was the only one.

At home again, muddy and tired, I set all the books from the library out on my bed. Maybe there was something I'd missed. Flicker flew over and started scratching at the covers, but I didn't think Mrs. Olive would be too happy about that, so I found him a cereal box to destroy instead.

I read until late, until my eyes burned with trying to keep them open. Finally I gave in and wriggled down under the covers.

I loved nighttime with Flicker, and not just because there wasn't so much poop and mess to clean up. You see, when I lay in bed, he left the toy box and curled up against me. I draped my bathrobe over him, just in case Mom or Dad peeked into my room, and lay there with him, listening to the murmurs he made while he slept, almost like a cat purring.

I slept so soundly with him beside me, and I had fantastic dreams, too. I dreamed about flying over icy glaciers, with volcanoes erupting below me and ice storms swirling across the open land. The dreams were so vivid that I woke up remembering every color and detail, as if I had really been there. I always woke up with such a happy feeling. And sometimes when I opened my eyes and saw Flicker curled up, he was changing color in flashes, one after the other, as if he was dreaming a happy dream, too. His scales rippled from red to orange to blue to white, pulsing like a fiery kaleidoscope.

That night though, I woke up with a shiver. There was no warming breath across my chest. Flicker wasn't on the bed. I peered across the shadowy room, waiting for my eyes to adjust, searching for the glow of the little dragon.

I finally spotted him perched on the windowsill. No wonder I hadn't seen him right away; he seemed to have turned a dusky charcoal gray in the darkness. I tiptoed over. He was staring out at the inky sky and the rain that was falling.

"Flicker," I whispered. He swung his head around and saw me and a little wave of color rippled down his body. He turned back, took one last look at the sky, then stretched his wings and flew up to my shoulder. As I scratched his head, the clouds parted and the moon cast its light into the room. I smiled as his scales shimmered their familiar ruby red.

I wondered what he'd been looking at. Was he searching for other dragons, too? I still didn't know if there really had been dragons in all those fruit. I'd tried to look earlier, but Grandad had kept me too busy. Seeing Flicker staring out like that, I decided it was time to find out once and for all.

16
Bat Watch

I had a plan. I was going to tell Grandad I was doing a project on bats at school and that I wanted to come over and do a Bat Watch in his garden. Grandad would have done his jobs for the day and hopefully be ready to put his feet up and take it easy. So I'd be able to have a good look at the tree and have a proper hunt for dragons. And as for Grim—I just had to hope he'd be taking it easy, too.

The next evening, I arrived at Nana and Grandad's fully prepared. In true undercover style, I'd brought my night-vision goggles, binoculars, clipboard, and a book on bats. I was almost beginning to believe in the bat project myself! Of course it nearly backfired when Grandad started reeling off facts about the habits of our native bats and got so into the idea he decided he'd come and join me.

"Actually I'm supposed to do the project without any help," I told him quickly.

"Don't worry, I won't do the work for you, Chipstick. I'll just watch. Scout's honor."

I shifted uncomfortably.

Any other time I'd have loved to be out in the garden with Grandad—we could be worm watching and we'd have a great time. But I couldn't miss this chance to look for more dragons. So I pulled out the only thing I knew would stop him in his tracks.

"I think you'd better take it easy, Grandad. You've done loads today." And then I added, "Think about your heart."

It was such a low blow, I winced even saying it. For a second he looked disappointed. Then in true Grandad form, he gave me a smile and said, "Right you are. Go on then—off you go so I can get back to *Gardener's World*."

Which of course made me feel ten times worse.

I hunted everywhere for the dragons, peering into and underneath the hedge, braving the nettles and battling the brambles. I'd seen Flicker dart out of sight enough times to know dragons instinctively hid from humans. Still, I'd hoped that with him flitting around in plain sight of me, any dragons would feel reassured enough to let themselves be seen. But despite that and my best efforts at hunting through the undergrowth, there was no sign.

Flicker settled on my shoulder and sneezed a glittering spray of sparks.

"This is hopeless," I moaned, nursing a scratch. "There's nothing here. Am I wrong about this, Flicker? Are *you* the only dragon?"

He flew up and ducked behind me. Eagerly I spun around, hoping he was trying to show me something. He was. It was my smoldering bottom. One of his sparks had landed on the seat of my pants and was smoking! I batted at my backside.

I sighed. Maybe I was looking in the wrong place. After all, it was Grim's garden that had been messed up.

I turned and looked at Grim's vegetable patch and at the little lean-to greenhouse that was attached to his shed, full of tempting greenery. A new polytunnel was lying in pieces, the plastic shredded and the seedlings it had been covering scattered far and wide. Surely this was proof there had to be more of them? Unless Grim was right and it *was* just vandals.

"I need to have a closer look," I whispered to Flicker. I wasn't sure why I kept telling him stuff when he was only interested in demolishing Grandad's lettuces, but I had to talk to someone.

Before I could change my mind, I hopped over the little wire fence that separated the two gardens. For a second I had a feeling that I was being watched. I stood frozen, listening to the breeze rustling the leaves on the hedge that bordered the fields. In my mind I could picture all sorts of things lurking behind there, but now really wasn't the time to let my imagination run wild. I reined it in and reminded myself that the scariest thing around here was probably Grim.

I looked around, scanning the garden up to the dark house where he lived. There was no sign of him, not even any lights on. If I was lucky, maybe he'd gone out for the evening.

Flicker fluttered over to join me. He settled on another plant with huge leaves and started nibbling at it. I made my way farther into the garden, hoping my luck would hold.

It didn't.

17
Hey, Stinker!

I searched around the plants and beanstalks, stepping among broken pots and bits of polytunnel. If dragons really had demolished Grim's garden, then where were they now?

In the end that question only bothered me for about twenty seconds because of the low-flying cucumber. As I said earlier, cucumbers and dragons are not the same at all. And one thing a cucumber *definitely* can't do is fly. Or so I thought. Except this one plummeted from the sky, almost knocking me out.

I looked up just in time to see two shapes spiraling upwards over Grim's greenhouse. One of them was clutching what I guessed was a bunch of carrots. Glittering sparks lit up the sky and fizzled out around them. *Dragons*!

Flicker spotted them and, leaving the half-chewed plant, he flew up into the air. In his excitement, his whole body pulsed with ever-changing colors and the sparks that shot out crackled around me. He rose higher and higher, and for a heart-stopping moment, I thought he would follow the others, but a little way above the treetops he turned and, flickering orange and gold, he came back to me. He settled on my shoulder and wrapped his tail around my neck and it felt like a buzz of electricity against my skin. We stayed there watching until the two dragons were tiny specks and then disappeared altogether.

I was right! There *were* more dragons. But it was clear that after some initial damage they weren't staying long in the garden. Or even nearby. Not given the general absence of fires and chaos in town.

But where did they go? Where exactly did dragons live?

Unfortunately it turned out that was a question that was going to bother me for *a lot* longer than twenty seconds, and no cucumber was going to drop the answer on my head, either.

I kept looking, wondering if there were any more dragons hiding in Grim's garden. I tried to remember how many empty dragon fruit skins I'd seen. I needed to check if there were other dragons who hadn't yet flown away. Maybe I could coax them into Grandad's garden and prevent any more damage being done to Grim's vegetables.

I made my way over to his shed. Some material covering the window meant I couldn't see in, but I stared through the glass of the greenhouse at the tidy rows of pots, each one with a tiny shoot peeking out. They certainly interested Flicker, who flew straight into the glass several times before giving up and landing in a disgruntled and slightly dazed heap on a nearby branch. They were probably Grim's pride and joy, so it was just as well the dragons hadn't managed to get in there.

And then a dreadful voice growled from the shadows: "Hey! Get your snotty nose off my glass, you vandal!"

No prizes for guessing who *that* was.

I turned and saw Grim storming down the garden towards me, his black coat billowing out behind him.

I had to admit this didn't look good. Not good at all. Me tramping through his wrecked veggie patch to stand with my nose pressed up to his greenhouse. And I knew it, so the guilty look on my face can't have helped.

"Just look at my plot!" Grim snarled. "I knew you were trouble, soon as I laid eyes on you." He looked around at the devastation. "My poor onions and eggplants," he moaned.

Excuses tumbled into my head. Any one of them would have done, but in my panic, they all got mixed up so I ended up blurting out, "I saw a . . . fox. A fox . . . fly into your greenhouse with my football so I chased it away for you."

Grim glared at me, his face turning beet red.

Suddenly something flew through the air and landed at Grim's feet. We both stared at it, too surprised by the aerial attack to move. And no, it wasn't a dragon. It was worse. Much worse. Seconds later, the smell hit us, as the air filled with the toxic reek of rotten egg.

Stink bomb!

I ran, as more stink bombs soared around me and an angry Grim spluttered through the foul stink.

"What are you playing at? You stay away, d'ya

hear? I'll be watching you!"

As I jumped the little fence, I remembered the feeling of being watched and the noise of the hedge—it hadn't been the breeze. Or my imagination. I knew exactly what had caused it and who had thrown those stink bombs. Someone who had gotten stink bombs for Christmas. And it meant Grim wasn't the only one watching me.

"Stinker by name, stinker by nature," I muttered as I ducked down behind the dragon fruit tree. I waited till I was sure Grim had stomped off back to his house. There was no sound or sign of Liam, either. But the faint smell of rotten eggs still lingered in the air. That and something else, too.

I stood up, searching for the source of this new smell. It was making me dizzy with its heady scent. Then I saw something. The vivid tendrils on one of the long green cactus arms of the dragon fruit tree had parted. Nestled inside were the white petals of a flower. In the moonlight, it seemed to be glowing.

I remembered Grandad reading aloud from the book. How he had said that before the fruit, there came a flower that bloomed for just one night. I looked around. Several more flowers were starting to open. And then I saw one amazing flower already in full bloom. The tendrils had spread into a star shape and the moon-white petals  within had unfolded to reveal a golden heart. This flower was as big as my head. And I breathed in the rich scent of it, picturing the fruit to come.

Suddenly I knew what I had to do. With Liam nosing around and goodness knows how many more dragons soon to be growing on the tree, I needed to get help. I needed my superhero squad with me.

18
Nosy Eyes!

Once I'd made the decision to tell the others, I could hardly wait to share the secret. Suddenly I couldn't believe I'd kept it to myself for almost a whole week. They were going to *love* Flicker!

But at school the next day, it was precisely thirty seconds before I realized I had a huge problem. We weren't allowed bags in the classroom, and there was no way Miss Logan would let me get away with wearing my hoodie inside. Besides, even though Flicker still fit in my pocket, it wouldn't be much good if he started getting fidgety in there.

In the end, I left him in my backpack in the locker room. I hung it on a hook right at the back and put my gym clothes in front as a feeble disguise. I stuffed some lettuce through the zipper, whispered some reassuring words to the little dragon, and crossed my fingers he'd be OK till break time.

In class I kept trying to get Ted, Kat, and Kai on their own so I could whisper the exciting news. But we'd been assigned our groups and I was stuck with "Lions," while they all sat across the room in "Giraffes." There was also the problem of Liam's beady little eyes that seemed to follow me everywhere, so I couldn't check on Flicker at break. He was even loitering in the hall at lunch when usually he'd be first outside with the soccer ball.

"Meet me under the trees," I hissed to the others as I shoveled in the last of my lunch and cleared my tray.

"But I haven't even started my third sandwich," Ted said.

"What's the rush?" asked Kat.

"I've got something to show you," I whispered. "Something important."

"Well, go on then, show us," Kai said.

"Not here," I said. "Nosy eyes are watching."

"I don't think eyes *can* be nosy," Ted said through a mouthful of chips.

I ignored him and used some impressive eyebrow acrobatics to try to signal to where Liam was sitting, but by the look on Kat's face, I don't think it was working.

"You're being weird again," Kai told me.

"That's what I'm trying to tell you about," I said.

They all looked at each other and then stuffed the remains of their lunches back into their boxes. Apart from Ted, who just stuffed his into his mouth.

"Come on, then," Kat said. "It's about time you told us what's going on."

While the rest of them headed down to the end of the field, I ducked into the locker room. A quick peek inside my backpack showed me that Flicker was curled up fast asleep, his little head resting on his tail. I scooped my bag up and raced down to the trees.

"Well, then?" Kai asked. "Spill the beans. What's the great secret that's had you acting all weird lately?"

As I got my breath back, I noticed Ted staring at my backpack. It was bulging and part of it seemed to be moving about on its own accord.

"Er, Tomas, what's in there?" he asked, backing away slightly.

And so I told them.

And of course they didn't believe me. I mean, would you? I told them the whole story from start to finish and, dramatic storyteller that I am, I didn't intend showing them Flicker till I'd *completely* finished.

"Right, good one!" Kai laughed.

"Your stories get better and better," said Kat, smiling. "You should write that one down. Miss Logan would love it. But seriously, Tomas, what's really going on?"

Here was my big moment. I paused, savoring the deliciousness of knowing that any second I was going to see That Look on their faces. The look that said, "I just cannot believe what my eyes are showing me." And "Wow, Tomas, you are like the coolest human on earth."

I opened my backpack and reached in. All three of them began to lean towards me.

But just as they were about to finally see Flicker for themselves, a voice said:

"What've you got there?"

We all spun around. It was Liam. And his beady eyes were fixed on my backpack.

"Nothing," I said quickly, gently keeping ahold of Flicker and hoping he would sense the danger and keep perfectly still. He didn't; he actually sneezed and let out a spark that was red-hot on my fingers. I winced but forced myself to laugh it off. Kat, Kai, and Ted were looking bemused. I'd have to fill them in later. I turned and hurried back across the field. All I knew was that I had to get Flicker away from Liam's prying eyes.

But the little dragon had obviously had enough of being cooped up and was now struggling to get free. My backpack lurched from side to side as he wriggled desperately inside. I clamped my hand over the moving bulge, trying to ignore the strange looks some of my classmates were giving me as I hurried past them. All I could hope was that he hadn't done a poop in there, and, if he had, that it wasn't about to explode.

19
Coffee Surprise

No one was allowed back inside the school till the end of break, not even for the bathroom really. But by pleading and doing some pretty manic jiggling up and down, I managed to convince Mrs. Olive, who was on playground duty, to let me in. As soon as I was inside, I darted into the nearest classroom and fished out the fidgeting dragon. Once in the open, he calmed down and perched happily on my hand. He stretched out his wings, which flickered through varying shades of red, before settling into a rusty copperish color.

"Sorry," I said, "but there are too many nosy people out there."

Flicker fluttered down into the sink. It was half full of muddy brown water from the paint pots that had been left to soak.

"Don't drink that," I blurted, seeing him lowering his head.

I cleared everything out and filled the sink with clean water. Then I stood back, watching as the dragon drank and drank, swinging his head back and forth across the surface of the water to scoop up each gulp.

Nicely refreshed, Flicker took off to explore the classroom.

"Hey, come back," I hissed, keeping an eye firmly on the door. "Look, I'll take you out for a fly later, after school."

It was not the best time for him to be soaring around. I kept glancing at the windows, half expecting to see Liam's leering face smooshed up against the glass. But Flicker didn't seem to care. He was swooping and diving and turning somersaults above my head in a crazy display, like he'd just invented flying or something.

I tried to coax him back with some of Mr. Firth's yucca plant, but Flicker was having far too much fun to stop whizzing around for a snack. He dive-bombed towards Mr. Firth's desk, and with a gasp of horror I saw that, as he passed over it, he gave a little shudder. I was pretty sure I knew what that meant—I'd seen enough of them in the last few days.

And sure enough, I was right. Flicker had done a poop in midair! The explosive little stink bomb dropped away and I watched it falling as if in slow motion, down, down, down. With an even bigger gasp, I saw the slimy mess arc gracefully through the air towards the desk at the front of the classroom. And with a dull *plop,* the deadly dragon dropping dropped. Slap bang into Mr. Firth's coffee cup.

"What are you doing?" hissed a voice behind me.

I spun around and saw Ted's head peering around the door.

"Mr. Firth'll kill you if he catches you in here. Come on—it's nearly time to line up for the bell. Let's go!"

I looked from Ted to the cup, but before I could move, Flicker took off from the bookshelf where he'd landed. I watched as he started weaving in and out of a display of hot-air balloons that hung in groups from the ceiling. I held my breath, terrified his tail would catch on one of the wires and bring the whole lot crashing down. Following my gaze, Ted looked up. He was just in time to catch the dragon's next poop squarely on his forehead. The stinky green mess, which was particularly runny, dribbled down his nose, but Ted barely noticed. He stood openmouthed, staring in bug-eyed wonder at the little ruby shape flitting above him.

"Ted—meet Flicker!" I said, grinning.

For once Ted didn't say anything.

"I'd close your mouth if I were you." I laughed. "Don't want one of those little bombs landing in there."

Ted turned to look at me, his bewildered face still streaked with poop.

"But . . . but . ." he stuttered.

"Oh, and I would wash that off before it dries," I said, pointing towards the sink. "Dragon poop has a nasty habit of exploding."

A second later the bell rang and, startled, Flicker zipped down to land on my shoulder. I quickly tucked him back in my pocket.

"We have to get Mr. Firth's cup!" I urged.

"What?" spluttered Ted, who was desperately splashing water over his face.

"The coffee cup," I said, my voice now all tight and squeaky with panic. "He pooped in it!"

We didn't get the coffee cup, because before either of us could get to it, people started piling into the classroom and the bell rang again for the start of class.

"What are we going to do?" I whispered as we raced through the doorway.

"Hope he doesn't drink cold coffee, I guess," said Ted.

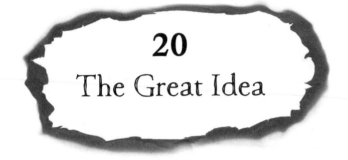

20
The Great Idea

Over the course of the afternoon, I watched Ted pass from dazed disbelief to almost uncontrollable excitement. When the last bell finally rang, he dragged me, Kat, and Kai to the corner of the park, to the little copse of trees where we made our den.

"Well, show them then!"

"Show us what?" asked Kat.

"Yeah," said Kai. "Dude, you've been off-the-scale weird all day. And now you've got Ted at it, too."

Ted was grinning from ear to ear, like the cat

who'd got the milk. And before I could say anything, he'd blurted out:

"It's true. He's got an actual real live dragon!"

Kat and Kai stared from Ted to me and back again, obviously trying to suss out where this setup was heading. Then, figuring they should just play along, Kai called our bluff.

"OK, then. Show us."

So I did. I opened my pocket and let the twins peer in at the glowing red dragon nestled there. His warm, smoky smell floated up towards us. And this time there was no talk of me telling stories.

There was a moment's stunned silence, and then—

"THIS IS THE MOST AWESOME THING IN THE WORLD EVER!" Kai shrieked.

"The totally awesomest," agreed Kat in an awed whisper, her eyes not leaving Flicker for one second.

And they weren't wrong. I stood there soaking up the glorious moment, the moment when for once I had the *coolest pet* in the world.

But Flicker didn't seem that happy with all the attention.

He fluttered up to my shoulder, curled his tail around my ear, and lay his head against my neck. I scratched him behind the horns, trying to turn the huge smug grin across my face into more of a look of cool casualness.

"What else can he do? Does he breathe fire? What's he eat? Is he going to get bigger? Where does he come from?" asked Kat, unleashing a tumble of questions.

"It's more sparks than fire at the moment," I said, laughing, "and he eats leaves and vegetables."

I didn't want to admit that for the most part, I was about as clueless as they were. They were looking at me like I was this expert dragon whisperer or something, and I didn't want to spoil that.

It didn't take Flicker long to get used to the others, and soon he was fluttering from hand to hand.

"He's *so* cute," said Kat, running her finger down his spiny back.

"Do you think he understands stuff?" said Ted. "I mean, could we train him, do you think?"

They tried calling him from one to another, and although once or twice Flicker flew onto the hand of the person that had called him, mostly he didn't.

"He's still a baby," I said, feeling like I wanted to stick up for him.

"Or as dumb as Dexter," said Kai.

Dexter was their terrier. They'd had ideas of training him to do cool circus tricks when he was a pup, but the most they ever got him to do was sit and stay, and now he didn't even really do that.

"Can he come home with us?" Kai said suddenly.

"Er, no," I said.

"Why not? You've had a turn. You've had him for ages."

"He's not a toy!" I said angrily. I made out that I was sticking up for his rights as a majestically free and independent animal, but actually I was overcome by a very deep feeling that I didn't want anyone else having the coolest pet any of us had ever owned.

"I didn't say that," said Kai. "I just meant we should share him."

It was true that we did share most stuff. Toys, books, games, all got swapped from house to house. But Flicker was different.

"He's mine," I said quietly.

Kai scowled. It reminded me of how Lolli looked just before she lost it. Of course Kai was old enough not to go supersonic, but I could see he was pretty ticked off.

It was at this point that Ted had his brilliant—or not so brilliant—idea.

"Hang on. Didn't you say there were others that hatched out of those weird fruits?"

"Yeah . . " I said, knowing exactly where this was heading.

"Well then, we could all have one, couldn't we?"

21
The Long Wait

After school, we were sitting around my room talking about caterpillars—Hah! Only kidding—I just wanted to see if you were paying attention. Obviously we were talking about dragons. Kat was poring over pages of library books while Ted and Kai were feeding Flicker green beans and laughing as he let out smoky hiccups.

"Have you read this?" Kat asked. "About the legend, I mean."

"Yeah," I said.

"But it's horrid."

"What's horrid?" asked Ted. "Flicker's exploding poop? Yeah, I know. I had one on my forehead, remember?"

"No, this legend. What it says about how when a dragon breathed out its last fire, it'd also breathe out a dragon fruit. But there were warriors who would seek out and slay the dragons, so they could present the precious fruit to the emperor as a treasure. It's so cruel," she said angrily.

The others nodded.

"Dragons always get a raw deal in stories," I said. "There's always some stupid knight stomping off to flush out a dragon somewhere, who was probably just minding his own business anyway."

Ever since my grandad had read *The Reluctant Dragon* to me, we'd never liked pumped-up heroes looking for glory. *We'd* both sided with the dragon.

We all looked at Flicker, who had settled on my lap. Kat reached over and stroked him.

"I hope they *were* just stupid stories," she said

quietly. "How could anyone hurt something as fantastic as him?"

"So you're sure these flowers mean more fruit is coming?" Ted asked for the gazillionth time.

"Yes," I sighed. "I'm sure. I told you, first you get those long vivid tendrils. Then over one night these moon-white flowers blossom and after that the fruit starts to grow. When they're red, they're ready to hatch."

"So now all we have to do is wait," Ted groaned.

I don't know about you, but I find waiting for something just about the hardest thing to do in the world. Imagine if Christmas, your birthday, and a trip to Disneyland all happened to be on the same day and you'd just been told you would have magic for that day and ride there on a flying carpet while being served free ice-cream sundaes. But first you had to wait. And you didn't know how long. So imagine yourself *that* excited. And that's about half as excited as we felt.

Every day before school, I raced over to Nana and Grandad's, hoping to see signs of the fruit.

And as I got into class, three eager faces waited for me. Every time I shook my head, it felt like I'd just told them someone had gone back in time and un-invented TV. And they weren't the only ones who were disappointed. I could tell Grandad was, too. He kept asking if I was coming back in the afternoon to help out. But ever since I'd told the others the truth, all they wanted to do was play with Flicker. And I didn't want to miss out on that.

At last, after several agonizing weeks, I ran into school. And I didn't need to say anything. Because Ted, Kat, and Kai could see the news written all over my face—like I had a neon sign there declaring it.

The fruit had come. And although they were only teeny tiny and nowhere near red and ripe, we all knew what it meant. We were officially growing dragons!

22
Operation Fruit Burst

Luckily for us, dragon fruit grows surprisingly quickly, and by the start of the following week, the fruits had reached the size of mangoes and started to turn red. The plan was this: We would ask my grandad if we could camp in his garden overnight. Then it would be simple enough to sneak down to the vegetable patch and look for the hatching dragons. My grandparents wouldn't even know we weren't fast asleep! And surely there'd be no chance of running into Grim in the dead of night.

Even luckier, there was a teacher-training day at school on Friday, so we could camp on Thursday night, catch the dragons, and then have an extra-long weekend to play with them. You really do have to admire our optimism.

So with Kat and Kai as our team organizers, Operation Fruit Burst got into full swing.

Planning is what the twins do best, and by Wednesday morning, we had provisions, plans, equipment lists, and an hour-by-hour timetable of the whole event.

It wasn't the worst plan ever. It might even have worked.

In the afternoon, as Flicker settled down in the toy box, scratching my latest comic book into comfortable-sized pieces for his bed, I looked at the list supplied by Captains Kat and Kai. I scanned to see what I was expected to bring. It seemed pretty thorough. You know, for just the one night.

PROVISION AND EQUIPMENT LIST
by Kat and Kai

SANDWICHES (Kat): Nutella & peanut butter/honey & chocolate spread/golden syrup with sprinkles

CAKE (Ted's basic collection): cinnamon buns, jelly doughnuts, fudge, cupcakes, Rice Krispies treats, Twinkies, Sno Balls, chocolate muffins, chocolate chip cookies, chocolate cupcakes, and chocolate brownies

Chocolate (Kat and Kai's birthday leftovers)

Emergency Chocolate (for hypothermia)

Extra Emergency Chocolate (for when Ted eats Emergency Chocolate)

Tent
Sleeping bags
Sleeping mats
Flashlights
Night-vision goggles
Walkie-talkies
Compass
Water bottles (filled)
Mallet
Bandages
Smelly stuff for repelling bugs
String
Woolly hats
Nets
Face paint

USEFUL BOOKS:
Camping in the Wild Outdoors
The Ultimate Survival Handbook
How to Survive a Bear Attack
A Hundred and One Deadly Plants

I wasn't sure where I was going to get half this stuff. The only walkie-talkies I could find were Lolli's Dora the Explorer ones, and I wasn't going to be taking those. As it turned out, the main thing we needed was the tent. And I bet you can guess what we forgot.

So there we were on Thursday, finally ready to put the plan into action. And yup—no tent. Luckily, Grandad had one lying in the garage, along with various bits of dodgy camping equipment, including some rusty saucepans that none of us felt like touching, let alone eating from, and an old lantern.

"We've had a fair few adventures with this lot, me and your nan," Grandad chuckled.

"Stick it in the front garden," Nana said. And then added, "That way you're nice and close for anyone needing to pop in to use 'The Facilities.'"

Which is her polite way of saying the downstairs

bathroom, which is just inside the front door.

So under Grandad's instruction, and in between his stories of camping in the wilderness, we put it up.

"Smells like feet," whispered Kat, scrunching up her nose.

"It looks a bit small," muttered Kai.

"And droopy," mouthed Ted.

"That's a good sturdy tent," said Grandad, resting his hand on one of the tent poles, and then quickly taking it away again as the whole thing sagged precariously.

"Good thing we aren't planning on sleeping much," murmured Ted.

By the time Grandad left us to go inside, we had gotten pretty well organized. There wasn't much room, but we figured being that close together would probably help prevent the whole hypothermia thing, which Kai insisted on reading to us about from *A Hundred and One Deadly Plants*. I'm not sure we needed to hear in such detail about the stages of frostbite, or to see all those pictures of fingerless hands. But as Camp Doctor, he was taking no chances.

"Right," said Kat as we huddled around the flickering lantern, "time to get camouflaged. Operation Fruit Burst is a GO!"

23
Attack of the Killer Leaf

I'd like to say it happened like this: We strolled down to the end of the garden, picked up a few dragons, strolled back, and had a good night's sleep in our luxurious tent. It didn't though.

First of all, the face paint we'd planned to use for camouflage stripes had dried up. So we improvised with dirt . . . only Kai soon realized he'd accidentally used the horse manure Grandad keeps for his roses.

"Well, it's better than dragon poop." Ted snorted.

"Yes, at least it doesn't explode," I added.

We tried, and failed, to stifle our laughs.

"It's a good thing," said Kat, biting back a snicker. "Animals won't smell your human stink and run away, so it'll help with sneaking up on the dragons."

"Go on then, you smear yourself with it," said Kai, who was getting grumpier by the second.

"If you want to escape a T. rex, you cover yourself in poop so it won't eat you," added Kat in a fit of giggles. "So if a big Mommy dragon turns up, you'll be the safest one of us."

I snorted so much at this point that the lemonade I'd been guzzling shot out my nose.

"Shh," Kat suddenly hissed as the kitchen light flickered on.

Grandad appeared at the window and stared out at us. A second later, he was at the back door. "Everything all right, Tomas?" he asked. "No one having second thoughts? I want you all bright-eyed and bushy-tailed tomorrow— I've been looking forward to having some extra hands in the garden."

Poor Grandad! I'd been so busy looking after Flicker, I'd hardly spent any time helping in the last few weeks.

"We're all fine thanks, Grandad," I said quickly. "Just, you know, having a stretch before bed." We all started stretching our arms up and running on the spot like we were in some manic exercise video.

Grandad looked at Kai's poop-smeared face. For a second his eyebrows furrowed, but then he said, "Okeydokey, sleep tight then."

I smiled at him. But the heat from the lie was already burning my cheeks—I just hoped the mud was hiding it.

We'd all felt quite brave talking it through beforehand, but when we actually ventured down to the garden, we kept a bit closer together than usual. And no one said much. We were all too busy listening.

Nighttime noises are freaky. Things that you don't notice in the day, like branches creaking in the breeze, suddenly make you twitchy. Every other tree cast a shadow that made it look like some terrifying monster was just about to jump out at us. So it wasn't surprising that we all shrieked in terror when a cat in Grim's garden made a high-pitched yowl as we passed.

When we got down to the end, we were all a little jumpy, to say the least. In fact, when a stray leaf drifted down onto Kai's hair, he started karate-chopping the air in a mad panic, shouting, "Something's on me, get it off, get it off!"

At which point we all leaped around as if we were being attacked—until we finally figured it out. At least laughing about the attack of the killer leaf made us relax a bit.

As we crept towards the dragon fruit tree, we began to realize we were not alone.

Strange dark shapes flitted above us, careening about, darting over our heads and criss-crossing under

the branches of trees. At first we thought they were bats. But when one of the winged creatures dived towards Kai, it soon became clear that they were dragons! A whole flock, herd, flight—I don't know, what do you call a mass of baby dragons?—whatever you call it, we had one right there.

I looked around at the others. Kat had her hands plastered over her open mouth, trying to hold back the squeal that was threatening to escape. Kai was standing and staring up into the trees, eyes wider than a wide-eyed lemur who's just sat on a thumbtack. And Ted looked like the cat who'd not only got the milk, but a huge bowl of sardines, too.

A few of the dragons were simply flying off up into the moonlit sky, but others had obviously decided to stop for a bite to eat. It was easy to see why Grim thought he was the victim of vandals. The dragons were not exactly bothered by the mess they were making. They had even finally found a way into his greenhouse and were happily demolishing the tiny new shoots. I knew exactly who'd be the ones getting the blame for that. Sparks fizzled in the night air as the little dragons darted from one plant to the next.

"Quick," said Ted, waking up from his stupefied gazing. "Get the nets."

We dashed around, fruitlessly trying to capture the flitting dragons in our fishing nets. But they were way too speedy for us. We staggered around the garden, tripping over brambles and landing in muddy heaps.

"This is no good," cried Kat. "We'll never catch them like this!"

She watched sadly as another dragon zipped over her head and flew up, up, and away into the night.

Suddenly there was a *THLUMP!* and we turned to see one of the fruits drop from the tree. A second later, the red spiky skin began to bulge and then, just like with Flicker, the fruit burst open and out shot a little gray dragon with yellow spines. Before any of us could get to it, it had darted away.

We made our way over to the dragon fruit tree and gathered around it, eyeing up each of the fruits still left hanging there. A handful of them were fat and red ripe. All we had to do was wait.

24
Here Be Dragons!

But as you already know, some of us aren't very good at waiting.

"Maybe we should pick them, like apples," Ted suggested, prodding a low-hanging fruit. "Maybe the dragons only hatch when they come off the tree."

"They have to fall off," Kat said. "You can't pull them off before they're ready."

"Why not?" Ted asked. "They look ripe."

"Tomas, tell him," Kat urged.

"OK, what did you do, Tomas?" Ted asked.

"Flicker's fruit just came off in my hand," I said,

remembering how I'd held it and gently lifted it aside, out of the way of the others. Kat was frowning at me, while Ted gave me a knowing look. They obviously didn't believe me when I said it had just dropped off.

I was sure I hadn't pulled it off though—at least I hoped I hadn't. I looked at Flicker, who was still almost as tiny as the day I found him, and suddenly wondered if he had hatched too soon. What if he wasn't growing properly because of me? Maybe this wasn't such a good idea.

Kat cupped her hands gently around one of the fruit.

"This one feels too hard to be ripe. I think we should leave them," she said. "Until they're ready. We can come back tomorrow."

"And hope they don't drop off, hatch, and fly away in the meantime, you mean?" said Kai angrily.

"If that's what it means, yes," Kat said sternly.

I could tell the twins were about to lock horns. I kept my eyes on the dragon fruit in Kat's hands.

"Wait, Kat. Look," I said. "It's glowing."

And not only that, the fruit was no longer attached to the tree.

"I didn't pull it off!" Kat cried immediately.

But before any of us could reply, the fruit started to bulge. A minute later, with a loud *POP*, the thing exploded. We stood openmouthed, splattered by a spray of fruity pulp. And there on the ground was a tiny purple dragon, covered in sticky, seedy goo.

Kat let out an excited squeak as the dragon stretched its neck and raised its long elegant head, sniffing the air. When it opened its wings, we could see shades of purple lightening into a beautiful electric blue. The patterns swirled like the tie-dye T-shirts we had made in art. This dragon had fewer spines than Flicker, but under its jaw

were spikes, hanging down like icicles. Quick as a flash, Kat gathered it up in her hands, delighted.

As she scraped the sticky pulp off her dragon's wings, Ted and Kai started reaching out to the other fruit left on the tree, feeling each one in turn.

"Careful," I cried. "Just be careful."

At first nothing happened; none of the fruits did anything. But then one of the ones Kai was holding flickered and began to glow. Kai's hand sagged as the weight of it fell into his palm.

And then, *POP*.

Another dragon shot out. This one was a vivid greeny blue with scales that glistened like the sea on a really hot day.

"Look at its wings," Kat whispered. "They look like peacock feathers."

And she was right. Although not actually feathers, the detail on the wings formed a feather design, and there were shapes like yellow and blue eyes leading to the outer edge, just like on a peacock.

Ted's eyes stayed fixed on the tree as if he was looking for the one perfect fruit. He reached up to squeeze a few of the redder ones.

"Ow," he yelled, drawing his hand back fast. "Rotten tree bit me!"

I laughed. "It's got some fierce thorns on it."

He sucked at the scratch, but since he had a mouthful of marshmallow, his hand came away covered in pink stickiness. Undeterred, he thrust his hand back in. It brushed one of the fruits and he stifled a yell of excitement as the fruit suddenly shone, as if his touch had turned it to gold. Carefully he cradled it in his hands, holding his breath. And then, just like the others, almost as if it had chosen his hand to fall into, the fruit let go of the tree.

Immediately it started to swell up, the red skin stretching under the pressure of the creature wriggling inside, fighting its way out. And then it burst, sending a spray of pulp all over Ted. But he didn't look as if he minded one bit as he held up a slender yellow dragon.

The shine from its golden scales made his hands glow brightly. He stared at it, his mouth hanging open. Not to get all poetic or anything, but if you'd been able to hold a bit of the sun, that's what I imagine it'd be like. Only without the hand-melting heat, of course!

Standing there, holding our dragons, we looked at each other with stupid grins plastered over our faces. I had to admit, it was going to be pretty cool to all have dragons!

25
Grand High
Dragon Master

If you think that four dragons and four people in a two-man tent would be a bit of a squeeze, you'd be right. It was a nightmare, in fact. The dragons had been quite sleepy at first, so carrying them back up the moonlit garden was a piece of cake. But it wasn't long before they started to wriggle and wanted to stretch their wings. Luckily I knew how to calm them down. Or I thought I did.

I'd told the others to come prepared with a shoebox and some broccoli and, because of my status as chief dragon expert, they'd all actually followed orders. I felt as if I could get used to this—my new role as respected elder, the voice of experience and wisdom, leading my minions. . . . Perhaps they should call me something like "Commander" or "Captain." Perhaps even "Grand High Dragon Master." Yeah, that sounded good. I'd probably need a cloak, or a special hat maybe, and a logo, definitely a logo.

"Hello, Earth to Planet Tomas," said Ted, poking me in the side.

Shaken out of my daydream, I saw Ted making his silliest face at me.

"Come on, Stinktastic, what do you think?" he said.

I waved goodbye to the vision of myself as Grand High Dragon Master. Who was I kidding? There was no way Ted was going to call me Grand High anything, except "Stink Master" maybe.

He was holding out his shoebox to me. And, I have to admit, the little imp called Envy started muttering away in my head when I saw it. He'd painted it in this really cool design, with bright shots of orange flame up the sides, and it was lined with a black silky cloth. Turning around, I saw Kat and Kai, cradling theirs. It looked as if everyone had gone to town on the decorating. Kat had a soft velvet scarf for her dragon to curl up in and the box itself was painted and covered in shiny sticky-back gems. A line of "rubies" and "diamonds" spelled out the words "Top Secret." If that wasn't guaranteed to make someone go in for a look around, I don't know what would! Kai, who tended to have a lot less patience for arts and crafts stuff, had just painted his a dark green, but even he had decked it out with some kind of fleecy material. They all looked way more inviting than Flicker's shoebox.

"Right, cool," I said, feeling pretty pleased that I'd managed to ignore my little envious imp who had been all ready to stomp off in a huff at having been outdone. I was glad because everyone seemed really happy that I thought they were up to scratch. And then they started quizzing me on what we should do next. I guess I was still Grand High Dragon Master after all, even without a hat.

"Food and sleep," I told them. "That's what's next. Get your box and your broccoli ready."

Flicker flew down and tried to pick the broccoli stalk I was holding out of my fingers.

"Let's see if we can entice them in. If they're anything like Flicker, they must be hungry by now."

The dragons were hungry, but it was soon clear that Flicker was on his own when it came to loving all things green and sprouty.

Ted's dragon appeared to have a taste for, well, anything and everything. He'd already found and demolished a chocolate fudge bar that must have fallen out of Ted's pocket, plus most of its shiny wrapper, an apple, and some chips, which Ted assured us he had been saving to share with us later. The dragon was now surrounded by what appeared to be the remains

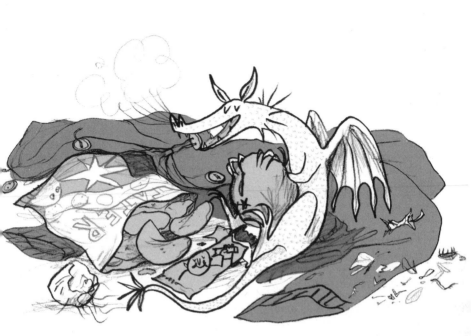

of several small insects and a hairy half-chewed marshmallow and was biting off and swallowing the buttons on Kat's cardigan. With every bite he took, his belly pulsed with a fiery orange glow that rippled down through his tail, as though flames were sizzling through him.

"Silly thing," Ted said. "He's just munched all our provisions."

"You're just mad because he got to them before you could," I said with a laugh.

Kat leaned across, trying to reach her dragon, who had settled by the edge of her sleeping bag.

"Hey, look at this," she said.

We peered down to where she was now pointing on the floor of the tent. All around the little purple dragon were patches of ice, the delicate crystals formed into amazing patterns, almost like the creature had been painting a picture in frost. The dragon stretched, drew back her wings, and let out another freezing breath, swinging her head from side to side to build up the icy markings.

"She's an artist like me," said Kat with obvious delight.

Kai snorted, but before they could launch into a full-on argument, I noticed something.

"Look what your one's gone and done, Ted!"

We all looked to the farthest corner, where there was a mound of what looked like cotton wool, but which we soon realized was the downy inside of Ted's sleeping bag. It had been ripped open. The golden dragon was now happily shredding Grandad's tent, its needle-sharp claws and teeth tearing into the material, and he had already made a fair-sized hole.

"How are we going to explain that one?" said Ted.

"Never mind about that," said Kai. "Where's my dragon?"

26
Poor Guppie!

We all stared at the hole in the tent. The dragon-sized hole. Making sure Flicker and the other dragons were safely in their shoeboxes, we crawled out of the tent and started hunting. But it was pitch-black now.

"It's no use," said Kat, after several minutes. "We'll have to wait till it's light."

"He'll have flown off by then," said Kai, in a full-on sulk. "Typical. Kat gets the artist and I get the escape artist."

We piled back into the tent, Kai still muttering unhappily. As we all squashed back inside, Ted suddenly howled.

"Ow! Stop it."

"Stop what? We haven't touched you," I said.

"Someone just pulled my hair."

"You must have caught it on something," said Kat.

"Ow! Stop it. That hurts." Ted rubbed his head crossly and glared at each of us in turn.

"Well, you can't blame us," I piped up. "You can see we're right here."

Ted looked around, confused.

"Keep very still," said Kai suddenly.

Ted froze in horror, obviously wondering what nasty nighttime creature Kai was about to save him from. He wasn't the bravest when it came to bugs and beasties—which may have stemmed from the time Liam dropped tadpoles into his milk.

We all sat there watching as Kai leaned forward and reached up above Ted's head, to where the lantern was hanging.

"Got you!" he said with a laugh.

And there in his hand was his dragon. Only he

wasn't greeny blue with peacock markings anymore; he was the exact shade of red of the lantern.

"Cool," said Kai, cradling the dragon with an expression of undisguised admiration. "Mine can go undercover, the ultimate in camouflage!"

We learned an important lesson right then. All dragons are not the same. Not by a long shot.

I wasn't sure how any of us were going to sleep, but eventually the dragons curled up in their shoeboxes. As the others settled down, I watched Flicker, his scales rippling through a kaleidoscope of colors. And then I must have nodded off as well, because the next thing I knew, it was light and someone was yelling.

"Is that your grandad?" Kat asked me, rubbing the sleep from her eyes. "He sounds really mad."

I'd never heard Grandad raise his voice, let alone shriek like that.

I shook my head. "I don't think so. Keep ahold of the dragons," I hissed. "I'm taking a look."

I unzipped the tent and peered out. Grandad was standing on the front step, Lolli tucked behind his legs in the open doorway. And planted in front of him was the fuming inferno that was Grim.

". . . Whole place trashed, that darn kid. I told you he was trouble!" he bellowed.

Honestly, that horrible man. How could he shout at Grandad like that?

I pictured the swarm of dragons we had seen last night. And how they had shredded, uprooted, and devoured whatever they could find before taking off and flying goodness knows where. Grim must have woken up and found the devastation and of course come straight here to blame me for everything.

Without stopping to think, I stormed out of the tent towards him.

"Hey, it wasn't us!" I shouted.

Lolli wriggled past Grandad and toddled towards

me. She wrapped her arms around my legs and clung on tight. With me off camping, Mom and Dad had dropped her off for a sleepover too, having a chance for a night out. But the rumpled frown on her face told me this angry, shouting man wasn't fitting in with her plans for the morning at all.

"Guppie sad," she whispered, pointing her finger at Grandad. "Poor Guppie."

"Now then, let's just calm ourselves down," came Grandad's voice. "It's probably foxes or badgers. Why not come in for a cup of tea and we'll see if we can get to the bottom of this, shall we?"

How he kept so cool in the face of all that yelling, I don't know. He deserves a medal, my grandad.

Grim was not so cool. He turned and pointed a finger at me as if he imagined lightning could fire from the tip of it. And I almost thought it would.

"Foxes, my foot! I've already caught him in my garden once. He was in there again, you can bet on that."

"What's this, Tomas?" Grandad asked.

"Didn't tell you about that, did he?" said Grim. "I told you he was trouble."

Grandad looked over at me.

"I wasn't doing anything," I spluttered. "I thought I saw something attacking his vegetables, that's all."

Grandad obviously didn't know quite what to make of this new information. "Well, like he says, I'm sure he wasn't up to anything," said Grandad, still keeping his voice nice and quiet. "And as for right now, Tomas has been camping in our garden with a few of his friends. They've been tucked up in their tent the whole time. Haven't you, Chipstick?"

Although I knew it wasn't us that had caused all the mess, I couldn't bear to look Grandad in the eye, not after we had sneaked out.

Grim turned his laser vision on my mud-splattered boots and trousers and then fired his lightning finger at them: proof! A look of triumph lit up his face.

Grandad's eyes dropped and also took in the

muddy evidence. And suddenly I saw his shoulders sag. Like he was one of those giant bobbing inflatable Santas at Christmas and someone had come up and let the air out of him, just enough so his head flopped and wobbled a bit.

And to be honest, that felt even worse than if he'd yelled at me. Because you know that twinkle I told you about, the one that makes Grandad's face light up? Well, it was gone.

"Honestly, Grandad, it wasn't us," I pleaded.

Grim glared at me and set off across the grass towards the tent. "Are the rest of them in there?" he growled.

The noise had woken the dragons and I could hear Ted, Kat, and Kai wrestling to keep them in.

Before Grim could pull the flap open, one side of the tent began to bulge. And then another. And then something shot out of the hole Ted's dragon had chewed. Followed by two more flitting shapes. Thankfully Grim was bending down, preparing to thrust his head in through the entrance, and Grandad had turned to scoop Lolli up, so no one apart from me noticed them.

They did, however, notice what happened next. You couldn't really miss that!

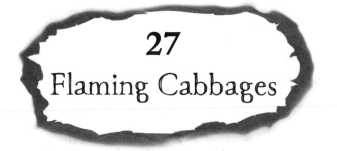

27
Flaming Cabbages

Having eaten everything edible *and* inedible in sight, let's just say the golden dragon had left a fair few dragon delights around the tent. And right then, several of them started exploding. There was a shriek from Kat, and then Ted came stumbling out of the tent, closely followed by Kai, who crashed into Grim. Kat crawled out after them, covered in dragon poop.

"That is truly disgusting," she spluttered.

But before anyone else could say anything, I heard a familiar little sneeze from inside the tent, followed by another one. Something had gotten up Flicker's nose and I could tell he was revving up for a full-on sneezing fit. Only this time what came out wasn't just a spark, it was an actual burst of flame. Talk about the worst possible time for *that* to happen!

I leaped back and the flames rocketed past me and ignited several of Grandad's cabbages piled up in a nearby wheelbarrow.

"They're playing with fire now, the little hooligans!" cried Grim.

I'd have denied it, except it was at this point that Ted's dragon, who had taken up residence in the blackberry bush, did an enormous belch and burned the heads off a bunch of Nana's roses.

"Pyromaniacs!" cried Grim. "They've got explosives in there."

Poor Grandad looked utterly stunned. And I couldn't blame him.

Ted scrambled towards the bush, but the purple dragon, who had been darting in and out of the lavender bushes, was peeing in panic, and since the pee froze on impact, it had turned the garden path into an ice rink. Ted slipped and skidded his way straight into Grim, who'd only just recovered from being tackled by Kai. Grim toppled backwards and landed on the handles of the wheelbarrow, catapulting flaming cabbages into the air.

This was too much of a temptation for Kai's dragon. Having turned a silvery gray to match the silver birch, he started batting them left, right, and center with his tail. I watched in horror as the cabbages rocketed towards Grandad and Lolli, who were now both ducking for cover.

Flicker flitted out of the tent and darted up into the leaves of a tree. He perched on the branch, eyes fixed on me. I didn't know what to do. The dragons were on the loose and I had no idea how to stop them. Kat and Kai were running around frantically bashing flaming cabbages with a garden broom and trying to distract anyone who might turn their attention to the little shapes above. Unable to catch his dragon, Ted raced over to help them.

But I just stood there, hopelessly looking from Flicker to the devastation unfolding around us.

Suddenly Flicker launched into the air, zipped down towards Kat's dragon, and began flickering like a beacon. It caught the purple dragon's attention, and with Flicker leading the way, they zipped back into the tent. Thank goodness for Flicker!

But there were still two more dragons causing chaos. Seeing Flicker reappear from the tent, I nodded towards the golden dragon who was belching flames. Maybe if we worked together we could do this? I grabbed a marshmallow from my pocket and threw it into the air towards Flicker, gesturing at the golden dragon again. Quick as a flash Flicker caught it, and dangling it from his claws like bait, he waved it in front of Ted's dragon. It was tempting enough to persuade the dragon back into the tent.

Now for Kai's super-stealth dragon. It seemed like this one was even keener to stay hidden than the others. Maybe if I could force him out in the open where he would have nothing to hide against, he would take cover in the tent. I waggled a leafy branch up at the tree to where I could just make out the little dragon's shape. I nudged him from his camouflage, and as he flew out, Flicker released an arc of sparks, herding him towards the tent like a sheepdog with a sheep. I watched as the dragon turned the same dark blue as the tent and then finally zipped inside. We'd done it!

But if I thought it was all over, I was wrong.

As Grim struggled to get to his feet on the icy

path, the tent began to rise up into the air. It swung from side to side like some kind of ghost. It was a very strange sight. And Grim obviously thought so, too.

"What the blazes?!" he cried.

Grim slid his way along the icy path towards the gate like a baby giraffe trying to skate. With his arms and legs windmilling in opposite directions, he fled from the flapping tent.

But it billowed after him and chased him out of the garden. I saw a flash of gold as Ted's dragon popped out and bit him on the butt, just for good measure. Grim howled but didn't dare slow down.

As we watched the tent and Grim disappear down the lane, somebody else ran out from the cover of the hedge.

"Hey, there's that sneak Liam!" Kai cried.

"What's he doing?" Kat asked.

He was bent over, clutching his stomach with one hand and shielding his head from the aerial tent attack with the other.

"What's he up to now?" Ted said.

"I don't know, but I'm glad he wasn't sniffing around earlier," replied Kai.

"Me too," I agreed. "But right now we have other things to worry about. Like flaming cabbages!"

Then, as if out of nowhere, black clouds appeared. An eerie light filled the sky. I remembered seeing something like it once before when we were on the ferry to France and a big storm blew up. Everything had turned a strange color. I looked over to Flicker and he seemed to be glowing especially brightly in the stormy light. Suddenly big fat drops of rain started to fall. With a sigh of relief, I saw the small fires around us fizzling out.

"Badragon-badragon," Lolli gabbled, jabbing a chubby finger towards the disappearing Grim.

"What's she saying?" Grandad asked, looking bewildered. He was still crouched over her, shielding both of them with his arms, unsure if the threat of flying fiery cabbages had truly passed. "Bad what?"

"Er . . . bad . . . ger," I stuttered. "Badger. She's saying she saw a badger. Over there." I pointed away from the dragons. "You were right all along—it must have been badgers causing all that chaos in Grim's garden."

Personally I think I deserve a medal for that level of quick thinking, under the circumstances!

"Ouchy," Lolli said. She pointed to the mess of stuff left behind from the tent. Grandad's lamp had smashed and glass lay across the scorched grass.

"That darned thing," said Grandad. "I'm sorry, Tomas. I shouldn't have let you use it. Nana always said the old thing was a fire hazard."

I almost gasped with relief. Without knowing it, Lolli had given us the perfect excuse for the fires.

"I should have listened to her," Grandad went on, "but don't go telling her I said so, or she'll never let me hear the end of it. Our little secret, okay?" And he winked.

I smiled. "Our little secret, Grandad."

I looked around at the scorched, cabbage-splattered garden and the tent now hanging from a nearby tree, dragon faces peeping out. Ted, Kat, and Kai were looking as relieved as I felt. I grinned at them and gave them the thumbs-up.

Lolli started tugging on my pant leg, so I bent down. She'd found a grass-covered marshmallow and was happily sucking on it.

She gave me a kiss, which was actually more of a nose slobber, but I didn't mind, because thanks to her,

the dragons were still our secret, and Grandad—well, he had his twinkle back.

"Good job, Lollibob Bobalob. Good job," I whispered. And she gave me a sticky high five.

So there you go. We all have dragons. And since you're still here, that probably means you want one, too. You haven't taken one tiny bit of notice of all the exploding poops, uncontrollable sparks, and general wanton destruction, have you?

Well, you can't say I haven't warned you. I can see you're desperate for a dragon and that whatever I say isn't going to change your mind. I know because I wouldn't have listened to me either, not when there's a chance of having a dragon of your own.

OK then. So, what have we learned?

First off, by now you should know what to look for. You *were* paying attention to that, I hope. You did take some notes about the dragon fruit tree? Make a few sketches?

Nope? Honestly, you need to keep your eye on the ball if you're going to keep dragons. All right, one more time then—look out for:

A tree with:

A knobbly hairy trunk.

Long spiky green cactus arms.

Weird sprouty mop-top.

Dangly great tendrils.

Red spiky pineapple fruit.

Got it? Good. Because that, you dragon-seeking desperados, is what you're looking for—*if* you want to grow dragons. Did you note the "if" there? Which should be a very **big** "IF." No, of course you didn't. You're already dreaming of all those flames and the fire-breathing and flying.

And who can blame you?

But let me just tell you this—I do know I was wrong about dragons being the coolest thing in the world. They're not.

Because Flicker isn't a *thing*; he's not even a pet. He's my friend.

Now that Ted, Kat, and Kai have their dragons, they'll get to see it, too. So that's what you can expect once you've found your dragon fruit tree and hatched yourself a dragon.

But after that, what more can you expect?

Let's just say *that's* something we were about to find out!

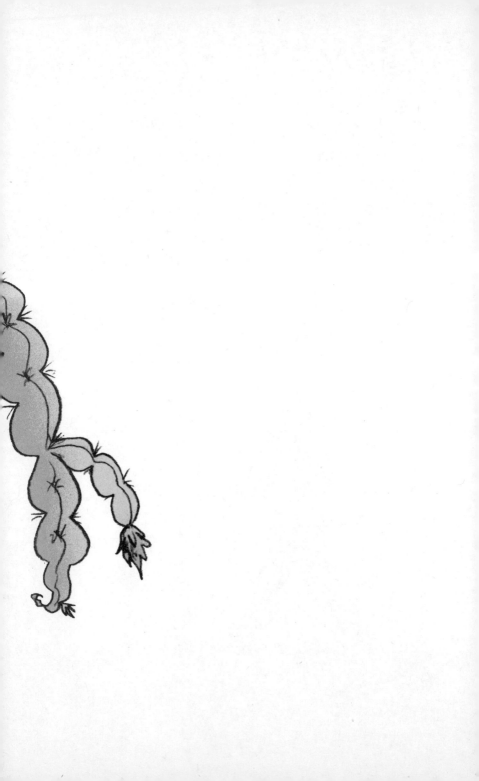

Acknowledgments

First off, huge thanks to Sara Ogilvie for her completely magical illustrations. I love every single one and should probably spend more time writing and less time staring at them. And to my agent extraordinaire, Jo Williamson, who never gives up. You are the perfect blend of fun and fiercely determined.

Thanks also to Tilda Johnson and Georgia Murray—the kind of editors I dreamed of finding. Brilliant, clever, and above all, kind.

Thank you to everyone at Piccadilly Press and Yellow Jacket for the excitement you have shown for this book.

My love and thanks to Mom, Dad, Pete, and all my lovely family and friends near and far who have cheered me on. Especially my own brilliant superhero squad— Bon, Tor, and Pam.

And of course, Ian. I'd need another book to list all the reasons. But here's just one—thank you for believing in me so much that I had to believe, too.

And finally, Ben and Jonas—my wonderful boys. These are your books. Thank you for always helping me find the magic.

Andy Shepherd is a children's writer working on middle-grade fiction and picture books. She lives near Cambridge, England, with her husband, two sons, and their border collie. She spends her spare time trying to figure out how to move this beautiful city closer to the sea. *The Boy Who Grew Dragons* is her first book. You can follow her on Twitter @andyjshepherd or Facebook at andyshepherdwriter.

Sara Ogilvie is an award-winning artist/illustrator. She was born in Edinburgh and now lives in Newcastle upon Tyne. Sara's many picture books include *The Detective Dog* by Julia Donaldson, *The Worst Princess* by Anna Kemp, and *Izzy Gizmo* by Pip Jones. Her middle-grade fiction includes Phil Earle's *Demolition Dad* (and others in the Storey Street series).

saraogilvie.com

nbillustration.co.uk/portfolios/sara-ogilv